Praise for

THE BEST AT IT

A Stonewall Honor Book

An ALA Rainbow List Selection

A Junior Library Guild Selection

A Chicago Public Library Best Fiction for Older Readers Selection

A Scripps Spelling Bee's Bookshelf Selection

★ "The protagonist's devastatingly honest voice pulls readers deeply into a fast-paced journey. Heartbreakingly authentic." —*Kirkus Reviews* (starred review)

★ "An impressive first novel: wholly engaging."
—ALA *Booklist* (starred review)

★ "This funny, uplifting story about identity . . . sends a powerful, positive message to young readers about choosing self-acceptance."
—*Publishers Weekly* (starred review)

"Rahul is a compelling protagonist. . . . Hand this to middle grade readers who are navigating changing social dynamics as they come of age." —*School Library Journal*

"Maulik Pancholy's story of an Indian American boy trying to come to terms with all facets of his identity while proving his own worth is at once exuberant and heart-wrenching, brightened with assured, lived-in details and a hero we love from the very first page. Every middle schooler will find themselves in this book. A wonderful, heartfelt debut." —SOMAN CHAINANI, *New York Times* bestselling author of the School for Good and Evil series

"An emotional, earnest, and genuine journey to self-love that had me crying, laughing, and cheering Rahul on from beginning to end. Hilarious and heartbreaking and truly touching—I wanted nothing more than to reach through the pages and give Rahul a big hug for being brave, determined, and the best that he can be."

—KACEN CALLENDER, Stonewall and Lambda Award–winning author of *Hurricane Child*

"A funny, fun, big-hearted book filled with characters to adore. Rahul's journey toward learning to stand up for himself and finding his place in the world is achingly emotionally authentic and deeply resonant. This novel is a joy from beginning to end." —ANNE URSU, award-winning author of *Breadcrumbs* and *The Lost Girl*

THE BEST AT IT

MAULIK PANCHOLY

BALZER + BRAY
An Imprint of HarperCollins*Publishers*

Balzer + Bray is an imprint of HarperCollins Publishers.

The Best at It
 For information address HarperCollins Children's Books, a division of HarperCollins Publishers,
195 Broadway, New York, NY 10007.
www.harpercollinschildrens.com
An In This Together Media Collaboration

Library of Congress Cataloging-in-Publication Data
Names: Pancholy, Maulik, author.
Title: The best at it / Maulik Pancholy.
Description: First edition. | New York, NY : Balzer + Bray, [2019] | Summary: Twelve-year-old Rahul Kapoor, an Indian American boy growing up in small-town Indiana, struggles to come to terms with his identity, including that he may be gay.
Identifiers: LCCN 2019009804 | ISBN 9780062866417 (hardback) | 9780062866424 (paperback)
Subjects: | CYAC: Identity—Fiction . | Anxiety—Fiction. | Middle schools—Fiction. | Schools—Fiction. | Bullying—Fiction. | East Indian Americans—Fiction. | Family life—Indiana—Fiction. | Indiana—Fiction. | BISAC: JUVENILE FICTION / Social Issues / Adolescence. | JUVENILE FICTION / Social Issues / Bullying.
Classification: LCC PZ7.1.P35743 Bes 2019 | DDC [Fic]—dc23 LC record available at https://lccn.loc.gov/2019009804

Typography by Carla Weise
21 22 23 24 PC/BRR 10 9 8 7 6 5 4 3 2
❖
First paperback edition, 2020

For every kid who's ever wondered,
"Am I good enough?"

THE BEST AT IT

CHAPTER 1

Chelsea and I are playing *Just Dance* in the basement when my grandfather, Bhai, calls down the stairs. "It's the last day of your vacation! You kids need to get out of the house!"

"Maybe later!" I yell back up. The song comes to a finish, and Chelsea throws her arms in the air and bows with a flourish. "We're just in the middle of something right now!"

"You've been locked away in that basement all summer!" he calls back down. Then his voice grows sly. "How about we have a race around the neighborhood?"

"Should we go up?" Chelsea tugs on her T-shirt to air out the sweat.

I love hanging out with my grandfather. I really do. But lately I've been avoiding playing out in the street. I mean, who wants to risk running into someone from school over the summer? Isn't nine months of the year enough?

"Bet I can beat you in a race from our house to Mr. McCarter's Jeep!" Bhai says, refusing to give up. Then he pauses and adds, "If you win, I'll teach you how to pop a wheelie in my wheelchair!"

I look at Chelsea with my eyebrows raised. Bhai's wheelies are pretty awesome. Plus, we both know he'll be home alone all day when we head back to school tomorrow. It'd be nice to spend some time with him. She shrugs as if to say "Why not?"

"Fine, you're on!" We clamber up the stairs.

"I call referee!" she yells as we follow Bhai out the front door.

Before we make our way into the street, I do a quick sweep of the neighborhood. Except for Dad's band rehearsing in our garage, it's a ghost town out here. Probably because it's August in Indiana and, like, two hundred degrees out.

The race is on.

I hop up and down to loosen my limbs as Bhai wheels in next to me. "Whoever touches the Jeep first wins!" He tugs on his wool hat and adjusts his cardigan, his eyes twinkling in my direction. Even though it's sweltering, Bhai never strays from his signature look. He has a Mr. Rogers–worthy supply of cardigans. I think all Indian grandfathers do.

"On your marks!" Chelsea's voice slices through the thick summer air.

I curl my lip and throw my best "you better watch out" look in Bhai's direction. The sun gleaming off his wheelchair stings my eyes.

"Stop! Wait! I can't see!" I yell.

"Rahul!" Chelsea suppresses a laugh as I bat away at the green and black sunspots dancing in front of my face.

"Sorry, sorry!" I shove my glasses back up onto my sweaty nose. The green lawns and giant oak trees lining our street come back into focus.

Chelsea runs her hands through her short blond hair and starts again. "On your marks!"

"One more second!" I bend over to fiddle with my shoelace. "I think this knot's a little loose."

Bhai raises his hand. "Excuse me, Chelsea, are there rules against this kind of stalling?"

"If there aren't, there should be." She shakes her head at me. "Your shoes are fine, Ra. Plus, my dad's going to be here soon to pick me up! Now, get set!"

"Hold up!" Now I've gone and untied the whole thing.

"GOOOOO!"

I retie it just in time to see Bhai fly past the starting line. He slams his hands over and over onto the tires of his wheelchair with lightning speed.

"No fair!" I yell, taking off. But he's already ahead of me.

"Very fair!" He shouts, throwing his head over his shoulder to shoot me a devilish grin. He bursts into a full-throated laugh.

Bhai has the world's best laugh. It's like two scoops of mint-double-chocolate-chip ice cream *and* a family trip to Disney World all rolled into one.

"I think your other shoe is untied too!" Bhai hollers back at me.

"Huh?!" I stop to look.

Chelsea facepalms. "Really, Ra?"

Oldest trick in the book. Bhai might be seventy-two and in a wheelchair, but he's competitive as all get-out.

I bite my lower lip and take off for a second time,

pumping my arms like a madman.

You might be thinking, how on earth could a twelve-year-old kid *not* beat a seventy-two-year-old man in a wheelchair? Well, you haven't met Bhai. He maneuvers that chair like it's a Lamborghini.

We also have an agreement: he doesn't baby me just because I'm twelve, and I don't coddle him just because he's got sixty years on me. In fact, he's the one who insisted I call him "Bhai." It's pronounced kinda like "buy" and it means *older brother.*

When I asked him why, he said, "Because you should always be able to tell me anything that's on your mind, as though I'm your older brother." Which is weird, because I prefer that my younger brother, Arun, not tell me anything at all.

I'm just a few feet behind him now, and Bhai whips his head over his shoulder again and taunts me. "It's just to Mr. McCarter's Jeep! You better catch up!"

"You're going down!" I scream, surprised at how out of breath I'm getting. How is he going this fast?

Dad's band down the street is scoring our every move, and the music pumps through my straining muscles. Chelsea is chanting, "Go! Go! Go!" in the background.

We're neck and neck now. I squeeze every last

ounce of energy into my legs.

The trees are streaks of green and brown on either side of me. I narrow my eyes onto the Jeep parked across the intersection of Oak Street: the finish line.

And then, suddenly, a voice shatters my concentration.

"Oh my God!" it snickers. "This has gotta be the most pathetic thing I've ever seen!"

Oh no. I know that voice.

CHAPTER 2

Of all people, why does it have to be Brent Mason? And why does he have to be in my neighborhood today?

Brent is my worst nightmare. The kind of nightmare that comes complete with splotchy red skin, a million freckles, dirty-blond hair, and a sweaty, hulking body that is way too big for a twelve-year-old. And, at the moment, he's coming out the front door of Justin Emery's house.

"Aaah!" he fake-shrieks, pointing at Bhai. "Help! Someone's escaped from the nursing home!"

Luckily Bhai is too far away to hear him, or Brent would get an earful about disrespecting his elders.

Brent ambles across Justin's lawn in a muscle T, annihilating patches of innocent grass with his gigantic flip-flops. A dandelion snaps in half underneath him.

"Hi, Brent." My voice comes out pinched. "That's my grandfather. And he doesn't live in a nursing home. He lives with us."

I look down at Bhai. He's almost to the Jeep now. Chelsea's screaming, "Rahul! Go!"

"I gotta go," I say, and start to take off. But Brent starts jumping up and down, raising his hand in the air. "Wait, wait, wait! I have a serious question!" he deadpans. "Would you call that thing that you're doing 'running'?" Then he doubles over laughing.

The screen door slams shut behind him, and Justin walks out onto his front porch.

I try not to stare, but Justin looks different. What is it? He's definitely taller. And did he grow some biceps while he was away at camp? Or is it just the football perched under his tanned arm that makes it bulge like that? He shakes his light-brown bangs out of his eyes, and I swallow.

"Yo, J., did you see how Rahul runs?" Brent guffaws. "This is what it looks like." He starts flailing his arms and kicking his legs around every which way. One of his flip-flops goes flying through the air.

Justin and Brent have been lumped together ever since the sixth-grade football team won the homecoming game last year, making them middle school heroes. So of course they're hanging out. But it's just my luck they would be at Justin's house today of all days.

Justin smiles at me sympathetically. "Hey, Rahul, how's your summer been?"

It's hard to imagine the two of them having anything in common besides football. They're polar opposites. Brent's a jerk and Justin is . . . well . . . Justin's *perfect*. Once, Trina Drexel literally fainted when he said hi to her in the hallway. He waited patiently by her limp body until the nurse came. Some say he even gave her CPR. A week later, they started dating.

I mean, how nice is that?

"Duuuude!" Brent gestures down the street. "Grandpa's going in for a crash landing!"

I spin toward Bhai just in time to see him throw his front wheels up in the air, whirl his whole chair around, and slam it backward into Mr. McCarter's Jeep. He throws his arms up in victory.

Shoot. I just lost the race. Because of stupid Brent.

Justin palms the football, holding it up near his ear, making his bicep bulge again.

I cross my arms to hide my own scrawny muscles. "Well, I better go."

"Buh-baiiieeee!" Brent says.

Justin tosses the football, and Brent runs down the lawn after it. He catches it in his stomach and body-slams himself into the ground, yelling, "Touchdown!" He wriggles his legs around like a cockroach.

Bhai starts wheeling toward us, and out of the corner of my eye I see Chelsea heading our way, too. Her hands are on her hips.

"Uh-oh." Brent heaves himself upright. "Looks like your girlfriend is pissed." He wraps his arms around himself and pretends to shiver. "I'm so scurrrrred."

"She's not my—" I try to explain, but Brent cuts me off.

"Yeah, I know. There's no way you'd ever have a girlfriend."

Then without any warning, he crosses all the way back to where I'm standing and squeezes his pecs together until it looks like the green veins on his neck are going to burst out of his skin. "Woof!" he barks. He throws his head right in front of mine, the effort turning his sweaty face bright red.

"What are you *doing*, Brent?" Chelsea doesn't mask her disgust.

"Nunya biz!" he says.

Chelsea rolls her eyes, but before she can say anything else, Justin interrupts. "Hey, what's that music coming from your house?"

I hear Dad's band down the street.

"That's Bollywood music, young man." Bhai wheels up. "Bollywood with a twist."

Dad and his two best friends, Vinay Uncle and Jeet Uncle, grew up in India listening to pirated cassette tapes of Air Supply. (Those are Dad's words, which always make me think of a bunch of cassette tapes dressed like pirates.) Air Supply is a 1980s British-Australian soft-rock band known for sappy romantic songs like "All Out of Love" and "Even the Nights Are Better," the lyrics to which NO ONE should ever have to hear their dad sing.

Recently they had the bright idea of forming their own band called *Bollywood* Supply, specializing in Air Supply cover songs. Except they sing them in Hindi. And to date, generally off-key.

"Bollywood?" Brent chortles. "Is that like, "YiYi-YiYi-YaYa-Yaaaaaaah? Ee-Ee-Ee-Ee-YaYaYaaaah?"

His voice is high and nasal as he flings one arm behind his ear and one arm out in the air. He waggles his head and his shoulders around in a really bad imitation of a Bollywood singer.

"That's not at all what it's like," Bhai says, his voice firm.

"Well, anyway!" I spin around. "We should really get going!"

"Brent's the worst! Why was he all up in your face like that?" Chelsea asks once we're out of earshot.

"That boy is a terrible singer." Bhai shakes his head. "Not to mention dancer."

As we walk up to our driveway, Vinay Uncle and Jeet Uncle are packing their synthesizer and tablas into their cars. Dad says goodbye to them and then tips his head our way. "Were you guys playing in the street?" he asks.

"I hope you kept your eyes open," he says before we can answer. "Some of the drivers around here have no concept of the speed limit."

Cars—as if. The real danger is people popping out onto their front lawns with no warning at all.

"We know," Chelsea and I mumble.

But Dad's on a roll now. "Just the other day, this high school kid came into the emergency room. Instead of reversing his car *down* his driveway, he accelerated it *up* his driveway. Into his own garage door. Can you believe that? So don't ever assume drivers are paying attention."

Having a dad who's an ER doctor means having to hear hospital horror stories on the daily.

"Was he okay?" I ask, casually peeking down the street to see if there are any damaged garage doors I hadn't noticed before.

"He was fine. But that's not the point, Rahul." Dad ruffles my hair. "The point is, you have to look out for yourself."

He struts up the driveway, humming a tune under his breath.

Chelsea and I let out the giggle we've been holding in. Bhai clears his throat. "Are you guys forgetting something?"

"What?" I ask.

"Oh yeah!" Chelsea grins. "You won!"

"That's right!" I bear-hug Bhai from behind his wheelchair. "Did you leave a dent in Mr. McCarter's Jeep?!"

"I hope not!" Bhai says, throwing a hand up into

the air. And Chelsea and I know exactly what he wants. We lean in for a BRiC, which is a secret high five that the three of us invented, named after our initials: Bhai, Rahul, and Chelsea. We had to throw in the *i* because we needed a vowel to make it a word. *I* beat *u* in a three-way tie.

The BRiC involves an up-top high five, a slap on the way down, a patty-cake swipe in the middle, dancing fingertips, and a mini hand explosion to finish it all off.

Some might say it's too much. I say it's perfect.

"That wheelie was epic, Bhai! Will you teach me how to do one anyway?"

"Why would I?" he chastises me. "You stopped running halfway through!" Then he smiles and lowers his head. "Although I would hate to give you both the wrong impression. You know that winning isn't what it's all about."

"We know." I nod. "It's about—"

"Just kidding! Winning is everything! And I am the winner!" He lets out one of his famous laughs, tips his wheels into the air, and then rolls up the driveway, leaving Chelsea and me shaking our heads and laughing.

We hear the sound of Mr. Wilson's worn-out

station wagon pulling up to the curb.

"Daaad," Chelsea moans. "You're early!" She acts annoyed, but aside from me, Chelsea's dad is her favorite person in the world. He's like the poster man for single parenting, and it's an undisputed fact that Chelsea's a total daddy's girl.

"I'm right on time!" he says, leaning out the window. "Besides, it's not like you two won't be together all day tomorrow. Can't believe you kiddos are going to be seventh graders already. Where does the time fly?"

"We're not 'kiddos,' Dad!" Chelsea sighs. "Well, I guess I gotta go."

"Bye, Chels."

As she turns to walk down the driveway, she makes her voice as low as possible and imitates Bhai. "I am the winner!"

We both crack up all over again.

Chelsea gets in the car, and I wave at the back of Mr. Wilson's station wagon as it sputters off, his bumper sticker reminding me that "Dinosaurs Didn't Believe in Climate Change Either."

When they're gone, I turn to look down the street toward Justin's house. From here, Justin and Brent look like tiny little action figures playing with a toy football. I've had a whole summer without having to think about kids like Brent. But tomorrow . . .

The front door flies open behind me and Arun's head pops out. "Rahul! Hurry up! We're ordering pizza!" He scurries away, leaving the door wide open.

I head inside and stop in the foyer. From the kitchen I hear Arun squealing, "Let's get TWO larges! Extra cheese on both! *And* cheese inside the crust!"

Mom laughs. I hear Dad say, "Arun, cheese is not a vegetable. You need to eat more vegetables."

I pull the door shut behind me and lean up against it. I picture Brent's Bollywood dance, and how his flip-flop flew through the air when he imitated the way I run. Tomorrow is the first day of seventh grade, which means I'll see him almost every day now for the rest of the school year. I feel a tinge of panic in my stomach.

I turn around and lock the dead bolt. Then I unlock it and lock it one more time.

CHAPTER 3

"RAHULARUN! LET'S GO!" Mom screams up the staircase, running our names together. "Let's not be late on the very first day!"

I check myself in the mirror over my dresser one last time, biting my lip and desperately trying to smooth my hair down. I practice a first-day-of-school smile. Ugh. Braces. One day, maybe when I'm super old, like twenty-five or something, these'll finally come off.

I grab my backpack and hoist it over my shoulder. I'm opening my bedroom door when I stop and toss my bag back down on the floor. I triple-checked it last night before bed, but I can't shake this nagging feeling that I'm forgetting something. I unzip the top front pocket. Three new mechanical pencils. Check. Two blue pens. Check. One red pen. Check. An eraser. Check. One container of hand sanitizer. Check. I zip it shut.

I unzip the main pocket. Two new five-subject notebooks. Check. Summer math homework nestled safely inside a manila folder. Check. Language arts textbook. Check.

"I MEAN IT!" Mom is relentless.

"Coming!" I yell back, forcing myself to trust that I have everything.

I barrel down the hallway, only to hear the exhaust fan running in the bathroom. I bang on the door. "Arun! Time to go!"

No answer.

"ARUN!" I bang harder.

Still no answer. I turn the doorknob and open the door.

Except that I can't. It runs right into Arun's fully clothed body. Passed out in the fetal position on the carpet.

He looks up at me. "Sorry, I was brushing my teeth and I got so tired I had to take a nap."

"NOW? You just got up!"

"But I'm still tired," he whines. "It's not fair. Why does school have to start so early?"

"Come on already!"

We both plop ourselves down on the bench by the front door and extract our sneakers from the shoe-filled cubbyholes below us. Like most Indian families, we're a shoes-off-at-the-front-door household. Bhai wheels in to hand each of us our lunch bags, and Mom hurries in behind him. She slides on a pair of heels and slips her arms into her suit jacket.

You'd never guess that she was up at five thirty a.m., had her morning neighborhood power-walking group at six, and that after she drops us off at school she'll head into the office to work all day. Mom's the CEO of this company that designs parts that go into satellites. Which means when I look up at the sky, even though I can't see it, I know there's stuff that she made circling the planet.

We quickly hug Bhai goodbye, and Mom's hustling us out the front door, when Dad comes running down the hall with his camera, topped by a ginormous flash, strapped around his neck.

"Hold on! Hold on! We have to get a picture!"

"Dad, we're late," I moan. "We still have to pick up Chelsea."

"You only leave home for the first day of school once in your lives!" He pauses. "Well, I guess twelve times in your life. Thirteen if you count kindergarten. *Actually*, fourteen if you count preschool. You know what? Who's counting? Get together. It's just one picture!"

One picture becomes, like, twenty, and then Dad makes us all do a selfie with Mom and Bhai in it, which takes forever because you can't actually see if anyone's in the shot when you turn a real camera backward. "Trust me, this is way better than using a phone," Dad says. "One day you'll thank me."

And then finally, miraculously, we're off.

First stop is Chelsea's house. Mr. Wilson confirms that he'll pick us up in the afternoon, gives Chelsea a hug, and then slides the van door shut behind her.

Next stop is Arun at the elementary school. He crosses his eyes and sticks his tongue out at us as Mom tries to plant a goodbye kiss on his cheek.

And then, finally, we pull up to a two-story red-brick building lined with windows trimmed in white.

Greenville Junior High.

Chelsea and I take the concrete stairs two at a time. My pulse starts to race as we enter the hallway. This is the same building where we had sixth grade, but somehow everything feels different now.

"If it isn't the inseparable Rahul Kapoor and Chelsea Wilson! Welcome back!" Mr. Hayden, our math teacher, falls into a quick step behind us. "Hurry, hurry. Morning assembly is about to start. Everyone's almost inside now. I trust you kids had a good summer," he says as he ushers us along, past rows of double-high beige lockers. "How'd you do on the summer math homework, huh? I've heard some grumbling that it was too hard this year."

"It wasn't that bad," I say. I picture the neatly filled-in packet tucked away in my backpack. I was careful to do all my problem-solving in a separate notebook, and to double-check everything. That way I could write in just my final answers and supporting work in a clean and orderly fashion in the packet.

"Speak for yourself," Chelsea grumbles. She half looks over her shoulder at Mr. Hayden. "That question about the number of jelly beans in Claire's jar was a bit of a bummer, to be honest."

"Well, if it wasn't a challenge, how would you

learn?" Mr. Hayden chuckles, pushing open the double doors of the morning assembly room.

Every morning at Greenville Junior High, the entire school gathers together in Baker's Hall before first period to hear announcements from Principal Jacobson.

The squeals of three hundred middle schoolers—"No way, you cut off all your hair!" "Your dad let you go to Six Flags? I'm so jealous!" "You got a pet *snake*?!"—greet us as the doors fly open. Kids are scrambling over chairs, giving each other hugs, and sharing photos on their phones.

Chelsea and I don't have phones yet. "Not enough research on all the negative effects!" Dad had said. "You can wait another year." Unfortunately for Chelsea, Mr. Wilson had listened to Dad.

We make our way to the seventh-grade section, which is a total cliquefest. We like to sit right up front, which means we have to pass, well, everybody on the way up. We're almost there when we run into a group of eighth-grade guys walking in the other direction.

"Chelsea?" David Nguyen says, waving at the rest of his group to go on. "Hi. Oh, cool. Love the button!" He points at the "Get Woke, Stay Woke" button pinned to her suspenders.

Chelsea just stares at him.

"So, what's up?" he says. "How was your summer? What'd you do?"

"It was good. Pretty good. You know . . . good." Chelsea rocks on her heels. "What'd I do? Hmm. Hung out. With Rahul. A bunch. My dad took me to a concert. For world peace. We camped."

It's like suddenly she's lost the ability to form full sentences.

"Very cool," David says, and Chelsea teeters back so far, I hover my hand behind her just in case she fully tips over.

"Hey, Rahul! Hey, Chelsea!" Jenny Ikeda, who's in our grade, comes bounding up to our group, her straight black hair pulled back in a ponytail. "How are ya?"

But before we can answer her, a crumpled piece of paper goes whizzing by us. We all turn to see Brent standing on a chair, hollering, "Oh heyo, wazzup!" He waves his arms in the air. Then he points two fingers at his eyes and then at me. Back and forth. Back and forth. "I see you, Rahul!"

Chelsea whips around and yells back, "Uh, we see you too, weirdo! What's your problem?"

David touches her arm, and Chelsea's face turns a light shade of pink. "Don't even pay attention to him, Chelsea. He's a waste of space."

The bell rings, and we all scramble to our seats. Principal Jacobson walks up to the podium. She brushes her tight black braids behind her ear and leans into the microphone. "Welcome," she says, "to what I'm sure is going to be the best school year ever."

CHAPTER 4

It's almost the end of the first week of what is supposedly "the best school year ever," but I can't wait to get home.

Turns out not paying attention to Brent doesn't really work. It seems like this whole week, he's everywhere I turn. And because this is my life, of course I got assigned the seat right behind him *and* his gargantuan neck in final-period math.

The squeak of Mr. Hayden's dry-erase marker on the whiteboard makes my skin crawl. He writes out "Join the Mathletes!" Then, with a flourish, he adds two underlines. "Any takers?" He whirls around to face the class.

"Bueller? Bueller?" He chuckles to himself. Our entire seventh-grade math class stares back at him blankly. "*No*body gets that reference? *Ferris* Bueller?" Mr. Hayden sighs. "Okay, never mind. But be sure to ask your parents about that one. It's a classic."

More blank stares. I feel bad for Mr. Hayden. It's not just that no one knows who this Ferris guy is. It's also that it's the last period on a Friday. Everyone is just waiting for the bell to ring.

Brent leans back in his seat. I choke on an internal vomit as I count the dandruff flakes floating in his tangled hair. One. Two. Three. Four. Five. Gross.

"Anyhoo"—Mr. Hayden claps his hands together—"as I was saying, I want you all to consider joining the Greenville Junior High Mathletes this year. I'm hoping to put together an amazing team. Maybe, just maybe, this will be the year that we finally advance to the State Mathletics Competition!"

A couple kids snicker, and I hear someone whisper, "Nerdfest!"

Mr. Hayden gestures to the wall, where it says "Math: The Only Subject That Counts" in cutout construction-paper letters along the top. Below that, next to Mr. Hayden's favorite "π, anyone?" poster, hang, like, a million certificates, ribbons, and photographs of past Mathletes teams.

But there are no trophies. Or medals.

"We've done pretty darn good," he says, and his voice gets all gravelly, like the guy who does all those movie trailers. "But we've never gotten to states."

Gina Carvallo raises her hand and asks if the Mathletes schedule will be the same as last year, because she's also considering Science Club and wants to know if she can do both. Now the whole class groans. Mr. Hayden tells everyone to be quiet, and then starts to answer her, but I don't hear what he says because Brent turns around in his desk and plants his freckly face right in front of mine. "You gonna be a Mathlete? Aren't, like, all your people good at math?"

"Um, actually, math's not really my thing," I say. "What about you? You going to join any clubs this year?"

A solitary dandruff flake tumbles out of Brent's hair and flutters ever so slowly toward my desk. I try my best not to look at it, but it's just too mesmerizing. Brent notices it too. We both watch as it softly touches down on my math book.

Uh-oh.

I fling my hand up to cover the page, but he's already seen it. There, on the top right-hand corner of page six of *Math for Everyone! For Seventh Graders!*, I have been doodling hearts.

Lots of hearts. Like, a series of little hearts inside bigger hearts, hearts stacked on top of each other, hearts with shading on one side of them to make them look three-dimensional. *Lots* of hearts.

"What the heck?!" Brent snorts. His arm shoots out and punches Justin, whose desk is right next to his, in the shoulder. "Yo, J., check this out. Rahul's in love with his math book!"

Justin peers back at me.

"I'm not in love with my *math book*." I bite my lip and shake my head. "Duh. I hate math! Doesn't everybody?"

Justin shrugs. "It's all right. It's just hard." He turns back around.

"If you hate it so much, then explain the hearts." Brent's breath is hot on my face.

"Brent. Rahul. Everything okay back there?" Mr. Hayden leans over his desk at the front of the classroom. "Are you boys paying attention?"

"Yes," we answer in unison.

Brent swivels back around in his seat. I wipe the lone dandruff flake off my book and quickly flip the page over. Then I lean over the side of my desk and unzip the top pocket of my bag to get my hand sanitizer. Who knows what kind of germs dandruff might spread?

"Good. Now that we're all listening"—Mr. Hayden shoots a warning look at Brent and me—"Gina, just like last year, practice will start off on Tuesdays after school, for an hour a week. Then we'll start doubling down in the winter to prep for districts in February. And *hopefully* states in March. And I promise all of you, you'll never have more fun taking a math test!"

He looks out at the class for a response, but the room is still blank stares. "Alrighty then. Speaking of tests, I've finished grading your summer math packets. So why don't I hand those out now?"

I'm putting my hand sanitizer back in my bag when a rubber band smacks me in the side of my neck.

"Wha?" I shriek as quietly as possible. I glance over at Mr. Hayden, but he's shuffling through the stack of math packets on his desk.

"Who were the hearts for?" Brent's turned all the way around in his chair again.

"No one." I sit up in my desk.

"Then why'd you draw them?"

"I don't know. No reason."

"There must have been a reason. If you're not in love with your math book, who are you in love with?"

"No one."

Justin looks back again to see what all the whispering's about, and I smile weakly at him.

"Wait a minute." Brent contorts his face so hard that all his freckles get rearranged. "Were the hearts for *Justin*?"

"What? No!"

"Why'd you just look at him, then?"

"I didn't. *He* looked at—"

"Oh my God. Gross. I knew it! You're—"

"Brent and Rahul." Mr. Hayden's voice surprises me, making my knees slam up against the desk. "Brent, if I have to tell you to turn around one more time, I'll have to move you."

Please move him, please move him, *please* move him.

Brent turns back around, and I look across the room to find Chelsea quietly waving at me. She mouths, "Are you okay?" I'm nodding yes to her when a stubby finger jabs me in the forehead.

"The hearts were for Justin, weren't they?"

"Brent. Shh. Come on, we're gonna get in trouble."

"Just answer my question."

"What?"

"Were the hearts for Justin?"

I set my jaw and don't say anything.

"They were, 'cause you're gay, aren't you?"

"What?" I dig my toes into the insides of my shoes. Mr. Hayden is two aisles away from us, still handing out those stupid packets.

"Admit it. Say you're gay."

I stare at the whiteoard.

"Just say it." Now he's hissing at me. "Say it!"

I can't take it anymore. "I'm not!"

"Yes, you are. Admit it, and I'll turn around."

"Brent!" Mr. Hayden throws his arm up in the air. Two math packets go flying out of his hand and zigzag to the ground. "Enough already! Face forward this second, or I'm sending you to Principal Jacobson's office."

Brent's jaw muscle ripples, but he keeps staring right at me. No one moves. The second hand on the clock at the back of the classroom *tick-tick-tick*s monstrously into the silence. Brent's upper lip curls ever so slightly, and a flicker of defiance flashes behind his eyes.

And then, finally, he turns around.

"Thank you." Mr. Hayden bends down to pick up the fallen papers.

Like a gift, the bell signaling the end of the entire school week finally rings.

"Hang on one sec!" Mr. Hayden calls, half the math packets still in his hands. "Let me finish handing these out." But it's too late. The whole class is making a beeline toward the door.

I pop up out of my seat, but I'm not fast enough. "Rahul, could I speak with you for a second?"

"I'll wait for you outside, okay, Ra?" Chelsea calls from the doorway.

Mr. Hayden waits until everyone is gone. Then he lowers his voice. "Hey, was Brent bothering you over there?"

"No. No. Not at all. We were just talking." I hoist my backpack up. "I mean, *he* was talking. I told him it could wait until after class. Obviously."

"Uh-huh." He searches my face. "You're sure everything's all right?"

"Mm-hmm."

"Well, in that case." He smiles and shuffles through the papers in his hands. He extends one of the packets out to me. "Apparently, I have to finish handing back the rest of these on Monday, but take a look."

There, in red marker, on the top of my summer math homework, he's scrawled a big "100%," followed by his signature exclamation point and two underlines.

"Your work was impeccable, Rahul! Excellent understanding of all the concepts and great attention to detail."

"Oh, cool," I say.

I roll the packet into a little tube in my hands. The last thing I need is for Brent to see my perfect score.

"So, what do you think?" he asks. "Are you considering joining the Mathletes this year?"

"Oh." I push my glasses up onto my nose. "Um . . ."

No *way* am I doing that. Can you imagine? I might as well morph into a human dartboard and wear a sign that says "Free Practice Sessions!" or "You Were Right: All My People Are Nerds!"

"You know, Rahul, in all my time teaching here, we've never gone to the State Mathletics Competition. But we have some pretty smart cookies this year. You. Gina and Jenny, who were on the team last year. David Nguyen in the eighth grade." Excitement starts to build in his voice. "If all of you join, this could be our year. We might actually make it to states. And it's a long shot, but if we win at states, we'd go to nationals. And going to nationals means a trip to Washington, DC, for the final competition. It's a *huge* honor."

I smile politely. "Well, that does sound, um, fun, but I'll have to talk to my parents about it." I turn to go. Then just as I'm walking by his "π, anyone?" poster, I turn back. "To be honest, though, I'm not sure they'll say yes." I suck my teeth like Mom does when she watches the news. "That whole Washington, DC, part could be a real problem. My mom and dad can be super weird about, you know, out-of-town travel."

"Out-of-town travel?" A dimple appears in Mr. Hayden's cheek. "Didn't they travel all the way here from India?"

"Yeah." I spin my finger around my temple. "Parents!"

CHAPTER 5

When I get into the hall, Chelsea is nowhere to be found. I head to my locker, and just as I'm finishing packing my bag, she comes running up.

"Hey. Where were you?" I ask.

"Sorry, sorry!" She looks flushed. "I was just talking to David. You know, David Nguyen? In the eighth grade?"

"Um, yes. I know who David is." I squint at her. "Is that why your face is all red?"

"My face is not red!"

"Yes it is, Chels."

"What are you even talking about? Why would my face be red?" Her face turns even *more* red. "He just said hi." We start walking down the hall. She scratches her cheek. "Although. I mean. I guess he's *sorta* cute, right? Some people say so, anyway."

"Um." I ponder it. "I like the way he gels his hair. And he's got cool sneakers." I catch myself. "Anyway, how would *I* know if a boy's cute? I'm not exactly the right person to ask."

"Right." Chelsea nods. "Right. Of course. Anyway, forget about it. What was going on with Brent in class? What was he saying to you?"

"Oh, that? Nothing." I wave her off.

"So why'd he keep turning around like that?"

"No reason."

We keep walking.

"Well, he must have been saying *something*."

"He was just being stupid Brent. Seriously!"

"Okay, okay!" She puts her hands up as we get to the parking lot.

We pile into Chelsea's dad's station wagon, both of us in the back seat.

It might sound funny, but carpools home with Chelsea are one of the best parts of the school year.

We bop out to Top 40 music while Mr. Wilson asks us a million questions about our day. When we get in the car, Pink's "What About Us" is already on and Chelsea and I are instantly in each other's faces with imaginary microphones like we're rock stars. We screech, "We are ro-ockets pointed up at the sta-ars. Pa-pum-pum. Pa-pum-pum. We are bi-illions of beautiful hearts." We're laughing and singing so loudly I'm pretty sure I'm going to lose my voice by the time the song's over. Even Mr. Wilson joins in. He almost misses the turn into the driveway of Arun's school.

Arun comes flying into the back seat, forcing Chelsea and me to smoosh up against each other. He slams the door behind him, making Mr. Wilson's Rosie the Riveter bobblehead do a little dance on the dashboard.

"Nobody's riding shotgun?" Mr. Wilson looks at us over his shoulder.

"Dad, we do this every day! You know Ra and I have to sit together, and Rooney's too little!" Chelsea says.

"I am *not* little!" Arun yells.

Mr. Wilson reaches back and tousles Arun's hair. "In a few years, you'll get to be my copilot. Now buckle up and get ready for takeoff!" He revs the engine, which is ridiculous, because it's just an old station wagon.

But I have to admit, I laugh every time he does it.

CHAPTER 6

Fridays, Mom works from home. She says she gets more work done that way because people aren't barging into her office all day long bothering her with a million questions. But I guess she's not working today, because, as soon as Arun and I walk into the house, the smell of Indian spices being fried in hot oil smacks us in the nose. The clanging of lids on pots and the falling of knives on cutting boards is second only to the laughter of my mom's six closest friends. Or as I call them, the Auntie Squad.

"Rahularun!" Mom calls. "Come say hi!"

We walk into the kitchen and mumble in unison, "Hi Nandita Auntie, hi Urvi Auntie, hi Mona Auntie, hi Nisha Auntie, hi Juhi Auntie, hi Purvi Auntie."

"Hi, boys!" the Auntie Squad calls out from every corner of the room: a couple aunties stirring pots on the stove, some kneading and rolling dough on the kitchen table, one chopping cilantro at the counter.

You're probably wondering why I have so many "aunties." Here's the deal: in Indian culture you basically call anyone your parents hang out with your auntie or your uncle. It doesn't matter whether they're actually related to you or not, and they certainly don't have to be your parents' siblings. The upside of this is if you ever forget if it's Purvi Auntie or Urvi Auntie, it's no big deal. It's just, "Hi, Auntie, good to see you." Or if you can't remember if it's Jeet Uncle or Mit Uncle, you just wave and say, "Hi, Uncle, you're really rocking those dad jeans tonight."

"Hello, Rahuuuuul! Hello, my little cutie, Aruuuuun." Nandita Auntie sails across the kitchen floor, her canary-yellow-and-hot-pink sari nearly blinding me when she lands in front of us. Before I can take a step back, she's leaning into our faces, staring at us through her Coke-bottle eyeglasses. One of her hands is covered in flour, and with the other she pinches both of our cheeks. Hard.

"Hi, Nandita Auntie," we mumble in unison again. Nandita Auntie's the only one of Mom's friends who still wears a sari whenever she can. Everyone else wears "Western" clothes. Not like cowboy-hats Western, but "of the West" Western. Which means American. Mom says Nandita Auntie's a little more traditional than the rest of them because she moved to America last.

"Hi, kids." Mom waves at us. She has an easel set up in the middle of the kitchen and a dry-erase marker in one hand.

"What are you guys doing? Don't people have jobs they have to be at?" I ask.

"I convinced everyone to play hooky this afternoon so we could start planning for the International Bazaar," Mom answers.

I look over at her easel, where she's made a bullet-point list:

- PLANNING COMMITTEE
- MARKETING COMMITTEE
- FOOD COMMITTEE

"Already?" I ask. Nandita Auntie pops a piece of homemade samosa into Arun's mouth, and another into mine. “Try this. You will like it,” she says, without really waiting for us to say yes. It’s so spicy, I can practically see the steam coming out of Arun’s ears.

“Isn’t the International Bazaar, like, months away?” I say with my mouth full of samosa. The flavors make me salivate.

“Yes. But we want to get a head start this year.”

“Are you going to be doing this every Friday?” I ask, savoring the last nugget of gooey, warm potato.

“I wish!” Mom says. “No. I have to work. But as it gets closer, we’ll probably start meeting once a week. Maybe Sundays.”

It’s cool seeing Mom run the show. Once, Arun and I got to visit her office for bring-your-kids-to-work day. She was right. People really did keep popping in all day long to ask her opinion on things, but they also stayed to joke around with Arun and me. Her assistant even took all these pictures of Mom and us sticking out our tongues and throwing peace signs so Mom could update the wallpaper on her phone.

“Why do you have to get a head start?” I ask.

“Because this year we want to do it right, so that people actually come. Attendance is always so poor, and we’re going to fix that.”

Mom writes “Entertainment Committee” on her

list of bullet points. International Bazaar (or as Chelsea and I call it, International *Biz*arre) is this festival that happens every year in Greenville. People of different cultures—and believe me, there aren't that many in Greenville—get together to sell food and gifts from their home countries while putting on a talent show. Most years, Chelsea and her dad make up the entire white-person quota.

Just as I'm about to reach for another samosa, Nandita Auntie pops a new piece into my mouth. "You need to eat more! You're so skinny! Are you fasting?"

The Auntie Squad erupts with laughter like a gaggle of hyenas. Indian aunties think it's hilarious to tell you how skinny you are all the time. And to ask you if you're fasting even though you're literally stuffing your face as they say it.

"Did you both have a good day at school?" Mom asks.

"Yup." I nod, my mouth still full. "Can I go upstairs and put my bag away?"

"But you both just got here!" Nandita Auntie whines. She plops herself into a chair and pats one of her knees. "Arun, *beta*, come sit on my lap and let Auntie feed you, okay?"

Arun trudges over. Nandita Auntie points at her

other knee. "And this one is for you, Rahul *beta.*"

I look pleadingly at Mom, but she's too busy scrawling in "Nandita → Flyer Distribution" under "Marketing Committee."

I reluctantly climb onto Nandita Auntie's lap.

"Oh-ho!" Her stomach lurches against my back as she chuckles up at Mom. "Are you putting *me* in charge of flyers? If I'm doing the flyers, you better watch out! The whole town will be coming!"

The hyenas erupt again.

"Well, in that case, we'll need a bigger venue than last year. Juhi, you're in charge of finding us a new location!" Mom scribbles in "Juhi → Venue Selection" under "Planning Committee."

Juhi Auntie has the world's quietest voice. Everyone has to lean in a bit to hear her say, "Why can't we just use the Greenville Community Center again? What's wrong with it?" She clutches her chest with her hand and looks so nervous that I actually think she might have a heart attack. I'm not sure she should be in charge of anything.

"Nothing's wrong with it, Juhi," Mom says. "But it only holds two hundred people, and Nandita just made a firm commitment to bring the whole town."

"Oh, right, of course." Juhi Auntie giggles, her

eyes darting every which way for approval. Beads of sweat gather on her forehead. "But last year, weren't there only, like, thirty people? Do I really have to?"

Nandita Auntie reaches toward Juhi Auntie, squishing Arun and me against the table. "You'll be great, Juhi. I'll help you. Now hand me some more samosas."

How Nandita Auntie is strong enough to keep both of us on her lap for this long is beyond me.

"I could probably feed myself," I say, trying to end this mortifying ritual.

"I know you can do it yourself!" She feigns being upset. "You kids want to grow up so fast, but you'll always be babies to me. You know who my first friends in this country were? Your mom and dad. And do you know who was by your mom's side right after she delivered you?"

Nandita Auntie's eyes actually start to water, so I let her slide the samosa bite into my mouth.

"Buuuuut"—she smiles and runs her thick fingers under her glasses, wiping her tears—"don't think I haven't noticed that you're growing up, okay?" She makes eyes at each member of the Squad, one by one, as if teeing up for the joke of the century. "I think we might have to start planning your wedding soon!"

It works. The Squad doubles over. Nandita Auntie jostles her legs up and down with laughter, and Arun and I have to hold on for dear life. Mom throws an apologetic glance my way.

I half slide, half fall to the floor, and Nandita Auntie grabs both my arms and looks me in the eyes. "Have you asked Chelsea to be your girlfriend yet? She's soooo cute!"

"Yeah, Rahul. Is Chelsea your *girl*friend?" Arun seizes the opportunity to needle me.

"She's not my—"

"You two spend so much time together!" Nandita Auntie's on a roll. "Should we go ahead and arrange your wedding now?"

"Yes, we should!" Arun is going berserk.

"Cut it out, Arun!" I scream.

"You know, Rahul," Nandita Auntie says, winking. "It's *never* too early to be thinking about marriage."

I can't get out of here fast enough.

CHAPTER 7

Finally, everyone is gone. In my room, I pull my plaid pajama pants out of my drawer and unfold them on top of my bed with a sigh. Somehow, I made it to the end of the week.

Parts of today were actually kinda fun. The Auntie Squad ended up making a huge feast, and then all their husbands—or as I call them, the Uncle Brigade—came over for a dinner party. Dad sang a couple verses of a Bollywood Supply song, and it was like 70 percent on key. Jeet Uncle banged out the rhythm, his head bobbing up and down as his fingers played the dining room table like a pair of tablas. Everyone clapped along.

Even Nandita Auntie finally let up on the whole Chelsea thing. She only brought it up once. "*Arre*, Anish," she said to Dad, "I told Rahul that it's never too early to start thinking about marriage. Next dinner, I'm inviting Chelsea's dad!"

Which, of course, made everyone laugh all over again. Everyone except Vinay Uncle. He pushed the bhindi masala around on his plate with a piece of paratha and muttered under his breath, just loud enough to make sure everybody could hear, "Let's *hope* he's interested in marriage someday, right Anish?"

There was this pause, then Dad laughed a little too loudly, and quickly asked Mit Uncle how he thought the stock market was going to hold up. But no one had even been talking about the stock market.

And then the moment was over.

Except that it wasn't. Not for me.

Somehow I felt . . . I don't know. Like I'd done something wrong.

I grab the towel hanging on the back of my door and walk down the hall toward the bathroom.

Downstairs, Mom and Dad are doing the dishes. Their voices float into the hallway, muffled by the running faucet and the clinking of plates. Dad's humming a tune, and then Mom must say something funny, because Dad laughs. Then the water turns off and there's a moment of silence.

I hear Mom say, "Can you believe Vinay? Talking about Rahul and marriage that way? Why would he say something like that?"

I bend my ear toward the stairs, straining to hear better.

Dad sighs. "Well, he might have a point. I mean, come on, Sarita."

"Come on, what?"

"You must see the same things I see," Dad says.

"First of all." Mom's voice is firm. "That still doesn't mean Vinay should talk like that. And what? What do you see?"

Dad exhales through his nose. "You know."

There's a pause.

Know what?

What does he see?

What?

And then the door to the dishwasher closes, like a cymbal crashing. The motor turns on and their voices disintegrate into muted sounds again.

I wait for a few seconds, but I can no longer make out a word they're saying, so I head into the bathroom.

I peel off my shirt and eyeball myself in the mirror. Then I ball up my fists and squeeze my pecs together like I'm the Incredible Hulk. "Woof!" I say.

I lift up my elbow and lean closer to the mirror and flex my arm.

Where on *earth* is my bicep?

I would kill to be Justin. Just for a day, even. I bet no one at his house ever says he's too skinny. I mean, why would they? He's *not*. He's perfect.

I slide off my socks, wiggle out of my jeans, and hop in the shower.

And what was Brent's deal today? And why did he have to see those stupid hearts?

I picture his face, and I scrub shampoo into my scalp so hard it almost hurts.

Someone bangs on the door.

"Who is it?" I yell.

"Hurry up!" Arun calls. "I need to go number two. I ate too many of Nandita Auntie's samosas!"

Ugh.

"You're disgusting!" I shout. "Use the downstairs bathroom and stop bothering me!"

And then, somehow, over the pounding of the shower and the whirring of the bathroom fan, I swear

I hear him rip a fart. "Yup. The samosas are definitely pushing!" He laughs.

I roll my eyes. How are we even related?

I turn off the shower and towel off. A blanket of steam has crept up over the entire bathroom mirror. I rub at it with my forearm, and a brown blur stares back at me. I pop on my glasses.

Still skinny.

I wrap myself in my towel and head back to my room.

But I stop in the hallway. It's like I'm paralyzed or something. For some reason, every fiber of my being suddenly feels like I need to check whether the front door is locked. Like maybe when all the aunties and uncles left, Mom and Dad might have just pulled the door shut behind them and forgotten to lock it.

And who knows what will happen if it stays unlocked all night?

What if something bad happens? Not just to me, but to everyone in the house?

A little drop of water slides down my ankle and into the carpet.

I need to go down. I *have* to check it.

But I don't want anyone to see me.

Arun must have actually listened to me for once and gone to use the downstairs bathroom. Light spills out of his open bedroom door and into the hall. The only sound coming from the kitchen is the humming of the dishwasher, so I'm guessing Mom and Dad have finished up in there. Bhai is probably in the living room, reading about Indian politics on his iPad like he does every night.

I tighten my towel and fly down the stairs.

I'm in the foyer. I glance to the left and to the right. The coast is clear. I claw at the dead bolt. It's locked. I unlock it and lock it again. Definitely locked. But somehow doing this makes a whole new wave of panic flood my body. I pull on the doorknob a few times just to make sure.

And then I hear the faintest sound behind me. Shoot. Is it Arun? I slowly peek over my shoulder.

No one's there.

CHAPTER 8

The walkie-talkie on my nightstand crackles to life like a three-alarm fire.

"Wha?!" I pop up in bed. What time is it? I blink to adjust to the darkness.

Glowing red numbers on my alarm clock tell me it's 10:02 p.m. A faint smell of dinner still hangs in the air.

"Rahul!" Bhai's voice blazes through the walkie-talkie so loudly the whole neighborhood can probably hear him.

I paw at my nightstand, trying to find the center of the sound. "Hold on!" I whisper, but of course he can't hear me. The walkie-talkie goes tumbling to the floor. I crouch next to my bed.

I push the Talk button. "What's going on? It's so late!"

"You. Me. Movie. Now."

"It's past my bedtime!"

"Who cares? It's a Friday night! Plus, nobody else needs to know!"

Bhai bought us the walkie-talkies for Diwali last year. Since the school doesn't give us the day off, Mom and Dad make up for it by going all out at home. They fill the house with candles and marigolds and paper lanterns in every color of the rainbow hanging from the ceiling. But the best part is Arun and I get so many gifts it's like a second Christmas.

Normally, Bhai gives us these silver and gold coins he brought with him from India. Last year, when he handed me the walkie-talkies, even Mom was surprised.

"When did you buy these?" she'd asked.

"I threw them in the cart at the store when you weren't looking." He'd coughed into his fist.

Bhai thinks of everything. They're the perfect gift because my room is upstairs, and he's in the guest room downstairs. Ever since his arthritis put him in a wheelchair, stairs are nearly impossible for him. This way, he can get ahold of me anytime.

I throw on my glasses and creep down the staircase as quietly as I can, tiptoeing to keep it from creaking. I edge my way along the hallway and then, finally, I'm in the den, sliding the pocket door shut behind me.

Bhai is already there, holding up a homemade DVD that says "Bhai's Greatest Bollywood Hits." He smiles. "Shall we watch our favorite?"

I break into a wide grin. "Um, yes, please!"

The den is just far enough away from all of the bedrooms that no one can hear us in here. It's the perfect getaway. The room is filled with a large desk and a super comfy couch. And there's a TV in the center of the built-in bookshelves. Starlight twinkles in through the big bay windows as Bhai pops in the DVD.

I hit Play on the remote. "Bhai's Greatest Bollywood Hits" is a compilation of Bhai's favorite Bollywood song-and-dance numbers from, as he puts it, the greatest films of Bollywood's Golden Age. Some of those films have more violence in them than Bhai wants me to see. So in order to give me an education in the greats, he recounts the story of the movie minus the violence, and then we watch the dance numbers from it.

When my favorite song comes on, "Yeh Dosti Hum Nahi Todenge," from the movie *Sholay*, I dance my way onto the floor next to Bhai. The title means "We'll never break this friendship," and it's about these two guys who are such good friends that one literally dies for the other. On the TV, the two actors singing the song bounce up and down and make goofy faces at each other as they drive around the countryside, one riding on a motorcycle and the other in his sidecar.

I dance next to Bhai, like he's in the motorcycle and I'm in the sidecar. We sing along, careful not to be too loud.

I throw one hand behind my head and stretch the other one out into the air. I'm bobbing my shoulders up and down when I remember Brent screeching, "YiYi-YiYi-YaYa-Yaaaaaaah. Ee-Ee-Ee-Ee-YaYaYaaaah."

And the next thing I know, Bhai is aiming the remote at the DVD player, and the screen goes black.

"Hey, why'd you turn it off?" I ask.

"Because you stopped dancing."

"I did?"

"Yes. You froze up."

"No, I didn't," I scoff. "Come on, put it back on."

"What's going on, Rahul?"

"Nothing. I was just thinking about something."

"About what?"

"Nothing. I mean it. Let's keep watching."

But Bhai sits firm, the remote in his lap.

"Rahul," he says. "Listen, as much as I love my greatest hits, I didn't ask you down here just to watch movies. It's way too late for that. You think I want to get grounded tomorrow?"

"You can't get grounded—you're the oldest one in the house!" I laugh, but Bhai isn't smiling. "Fine, if you didn't want to watch movies, then why'd you wake me up?"

"Because I wanted to talk to you."

"About what?" I get up to sit on the couch.

He looks at me, and it makes me uncomfortable.

"Is something wrong?" he asks.

"What do you mean?"

"Come on, Rahul. Remember why you call me Bhai? Is something bothering you?"

His wheels drag gently across the floor as he sidles up closer to me.

"No." I grab a pillow and pull it closer.

"Are you afraid of something?"

"Huh?"

"Are you afraid someone is going to break into the house?"

"*What?*" I force a smile, even though I feel a little panic. "*No*. Why?"

"Because I saw a young man wearing only his towel checking the lock on the front door and then running back upstairs."

My face falls. I knew I heard someone behind me. "Are you spying on me now?" I mumble.

"Rahul." Bhai's voice is so gentle. "I'm asking again. Are you afraid of something?"

"No. I just . . . I don't know why I did that. I was just making sure the door was locked. There were all these people over. And you never know."

Bhai folds his hands in his lap. "You couldn't wait to put your clothes on first?"

"I just thought of it, so I did it! Is there some rule now that you always have to wear clothes in the house?"

"Actually, yes." Bhai narrows his eyes. "As far as I know, you do have to wear clothes in the house. Tough break, but that's the rule."

I let out a small laugh.

"Rahul, is something stressing you out?"

"*No!* Nothing is." But I know I'm not being totally honest with him. "Can we please talk about something else already?"

Bhai sighs. "Okay, fine. What do you want to talk about?"

"Anything. Anything but this."

Bhai pauses. "All right, do you want to hear a story?"

"You mean like a nonviolent Bollywood movie story? Haven't you already told me all the good ones?"

"So how about something different?" Bhai rubs his chin. "How about this? Have I ever told you about when your grandmother first went to engineering college?"

"I don't think so." I perk up a little. I only met my grandmother a few times when we traveled to India, but she was so cool. I remember her taking me shopping for Indian clothes one afternoon, just the two of us. We zipped around in a rickshaw, the driver blaring his horn at all the cars in our way. At every store we went to, my grandmother would proudly say, "Rahul is visiting from America," and one of the employees would run out and come back with Orange Fantas in little glass bottles. I never drank so much pop in my life.

"I wish I could see her again," I say. "Do you miss her?"

"Of course I miss her." A glimmer of wetness pools in Bhai's eyes. "She was the smartest person I've ever known."

Four years ago, I was in the kitchen helping Mom put away groceries when her cell phone rang. It was Bhai calling from India. Mom answered, and then she got really quiet and left the room. My grandmother had been pretty healthy, but just like that, she'd had a heart attack and passed away in her sleep. A year later, Bhai moved to America to live with us.

"What happened at engineering college?" I ask.

"Well, this is a story your grandmother told me," Bhai begins, "because it happened before I even met her. You see, she lived in a very small town. A village, really. This was"—he pauses to think for a second—"about fifty-five years ago, when she was seventeen years old."

He looks at me. "Back then society was such that it was very unusual for girls to go to engineering school. Many girls, especially in villages, didn't have the opportunity to go to college at all." Bhai shakes his head in disgust. Then, his eyes twinkle.

"But your grandmother was determined to become an engineer. She worked very hard, and she got only the best grades. And when she got accepted to engineering school, every single person in her village came to the train station to see her off. They were so proud of her."

Bhai adjusts the blanket covering his legs. "Now, when she got to the college, she didn't expect that after all that hard work, she would get the treatment that she did. You see, the boys in the college were such backward thinkers that they didn't like having a girl in their class." He clicks his tongue, as though the thought of it makes him sick. "They made her life very difficult. If she missed a class, they would give her wrong notes from the lecture. If they were having a study group, they wouldn't invite her. If there was going to be some kind of a party, they would whisper about it behind her back so she wouldn't know."

Sounds like Brent would have fit right in with these guys.

"But she didn't let it stop her. She put her head down and kept studying. And wouldn't you know? While everyone else was busy trying to make her feel bad, who do you think got the highest marks in the class?"

"She did?"

"That's right." He nods. "One day, a Mr. Ramdas from a top engineering firm came to visit her class. He wanted to hire one of the students for an internship, and every student wanted to be chosen. So, this Mr. Ramdas asks the professor, 'Who is your top student? I've been instructed to hire the best.' Well, the professor hesitated, because he was just like everyone else. He didn't think a girl should get the job. So the professor said, 'Mr. Ramdas, sir, why don't you take Nakul? He's the number-two student, but believe me, he's a much better choice for you than our number-one student.'

"Mr. Ramdas said, 'But who is your number-one student? My boss wants the best.' The whole class was covering their mouths, trying not to giggle. Mr. Ramdas was confused. 'What is so funny to all of you?' One of the students raised his hand. 'Mr. Ramdas, sir, trust us. You will not want to hire the number-one student.' Now people weren't even trying to hide it anymore. They were clapping each other on the back and laughing in your grandmother's face. Mr. Ramdas banged his fist on the desk. 'I demand to know who the number-one student in this class is!'"

Bhai gazes up over my head, and I've never seen

him look so proud. "Your grandmother stood up at her desk and a hush fell over the whole classroom. Her voice was clear and steady. 'Sir, I am the number-one student, and I would be honored to work for you.'"

Bhai takes a deep breath. "The whole class went completely still. A girl enrolling in engineering college was one thing, but now she was daring to take a job? To speak out of turn? Every student stared at Mr. Ramdas, waiting to see how he would respond.

"Well, even Mr. Ramdas was shocked. He stammered a bit, but your grandmother remained calm, with her head held high. And then, to everyone's surprise, he extended his arm. 'The honor would be all ours.'"

Bhai pauses, and for a second it feels like my grandmother is actually in the room with us. He shakes his head and chuckles. "Suddenly, everyone wanted to be your grandmother's best friend. They didn't want her to just participate in the study groups, they wanted her to run them. She wasn't just invited to the parties, they were thrown in her honor! She commanded everybody's respect."

I'm so wrapped up in the story, I'm forgetting to breathe. Bhai leans in. "Your grandmother taught me no one can stand in your way. If you dedicate yourself to something and become the best at it, then nobody can stop you."

The moonlight streaming in from the window casts Bhai's body into silhouette, and the little wisps of hair peeking out from under his hat glow silver against his temples.

"Hey!" Arun barges into the room, startling the both of us. "What's going on in here?"

"Ugh. Nothing!" I throw the pillow from my lap at him. "Why are you up? You should be in bed!"

"*You* should be in bed!" He sticks his tongue out at me.

"Fine," I sigh. "Come on, Arun. I was just leaving anyway." We say good night to Bhai and walk back up the stairs, my brain racing. When I get to my room, I lie in bed and stare up at the ceiling.

I know exactly what I have to do.

CHAPTER 9

Except for a breeze ruffling the leaves in the giant elm tree in our front yard, the whole neighborhood is surprisingly quiet for such a nice Sunday afternoon.

I guess nobody else got the e-blast that today is, in fact, the first day of the rest of my life.

I couldn't wait inside for Chelsea any longer. So I got everything ready, and now I'm pacing up and down on the curb like it's a balance beam. I've got one eye keeping a lookout for Mr. Wilson's car, and the other trained down the street on Justin's house for any signs of alien life. And by *alien*, I mean Brent.

So far, no extraterrestrial sightings.

The garage door rumbles to life behind me and I jump off the curb to watch it. It rises like a curtain, revealing Dad kneeling over an amplifier. He's holding two split ends of a long auxiliary cable in his hand. His forehead has, like, seven wrinkles in it, and he's biting his lower lip. I hop back up on the curb, teetering on one leg.

"What are you up to?" I ask.

"Ah!" Dad claps his hand to his chest. "Rahul! Please don't sneak up on me like that!"

I'm about to say, "I was here first," but he's already buried in the cable again. His eyes dart back and forth between the two ends. "I'm setting up for band rehearsal," he says as he plugs one end of the cord into a speaker. It feedbacks so hard that somewhere in the neighborhood a dog starts howling. Two birds fly out of our elm tree.

"Anish! Not so loud, please!" Mom yells from inside the house. "I'm trying to work!"

"Sorry! Wrong end!" Dad pulls out the cord. Bollywood Supply just ordered some new band equipment, and I guess they're still figuring it all out. Dad plugs in the other end of the cable. No feedback. He reaches over his shoulder and pats himself on the back.

He walks over to the microphone stand in the center of the garage and leans in. "Test. One, two, three. Test. One, two, three." The noise boomerangs all over the garage. I cast a glance down the street at Justin's house.

Still no signs of unintelligent life.

"Are you guys practicing *again* today?" I ask. I plant one foot on the curb and do my best Karate Kid crane kick.

"Of course, every Sunday. Practice makes perfect!" He unfolds some sheet music onto a music stand and then starts unraveling another cord. "You know your Mona Auntie signed us up for entertainment at the International Bazaar, right?"

I hear Mr. Wilson's station wagon coming down the street. "Chelsea!" I yell. I jump up and down, waving at her, and she throws double peace signs at me through the windshield. She runs out of the door before the car even comes to a stop in the driveway. Mr. Wilson leans across the passenger seat. "I'll come get you in a few hours. Have fun!"

"You know we will! Ain't no party like a Rahul and Chelsea party!" We shimmy our shoulders.

I grab Chelsea's arm. "Come on! Let's go inside! We have so much to do!"

"To do? What do you mean? Hi, Dr. Kapoor!" Chelsea waves at Dad.

"Hi, Chelsea!" Dad grins. He strums his guitar and starts singing. "*Yahan hain hum, jisse chahate ho tum!*"

"Times like this I really wish I knew Hindi. Tell me what that means," Chelsea pleads.

"Ew! Ew! Ew! DAAAAAD!" I shake my arms, trying to fling off the grossness. "It means, 'Here I am, the one that you LOVE!'"

Chelsea and I are in each other's faces shrieking now. "Groooooss!"

"What is wrong with you kids? It's one of Air Supply's greatest hits! It's a classic!" Dad tries to explain, but Chelsea and I are out.

I yank her in through the front door, past Mom on her laptop in the dining room, right by Bhai watching TV in the living room, and away from the earthquake that is Arun bouncing off the walls in his bedroom above us. I fling open the door to the basement, and we dive down the stairs to safety.

"Whoa. What's all this?" Chelsea's jaw drops.

I've shoved away the coffee table to make room for Mom's easel, which is teetering precariously on the shag rug. Two beanbags are arranged in front of the easel, and I've laid out some notebooks and boxes of colored pencils.

I also raided the kitchen for a ton of snacks and bottled waters. This could take a while.

At the top of the easel, written in purple wipe-off marker, it says, "Rahul Kapoor's Quest to Be: The. Best. At. It."

I walk up to the easel with a big smile. "Whaddya think? Will you help me?"

"With what?" Chelsea asks, reading the board. "The best at it?" She keeps reading. "A planning committee? What's going on?"

I erased all the other stuff Mom and the aunties had written on the board, but I decided to keep "Planning Committee" intact. I figure this will take some planning, and Mom says committees are the way to get things done.

"A planning committee is how I'm going to be the best at it. And you," I say, uncapping a marker, "are my first volunteer."

Chelsea smirks. "Um, last I checked, I'm the only volunteer here." She reaches for a cookie and plops into a beanbag. "What is all this?"

"Okay." I take a deep breath. "Listen. This year, I need to be the best at something. Like, better than everyone else."

"That's kind of the definition of *best.*" Chelsea nods. "Go on."

"But, I'm just . . . I don't know what that thing should be. I mean, there's stuff I'm good at, sure, like I get good grades, but that's not what I mean. I need to find something . . ." I suck my teeth. "I don't know. Something that will surprise people."

"Okay . . ." Chelsea eyes me.

"And then"—I point to the easel—"I have to figure out how to be the best at it."

Chelsea chews on the inside of her lip. "Well, first of all, I don't think you need a planning committee for this." She furrows her brow. "I mean, Ra, don't people just do things they *like* to do, and then the more they do them, the better they get at them?"

"Maybe. But better's not good enough. I've got to be the *best*. Also, I need to do it fast."

"What's the big rush?"

The door to the basement squeaks open.

"Hi, kids." Mom makes her way down with a plate of nachos. "I thought you guys might want a snack."

I fling my arms up over my head and pretend

to yawn, doing my best to block the easel. For some reason, I don't want to have to explain all this to her.

She notices the food I've laid out. "Oh, I didn't realize you already brought so much stuff down. I wouldn't have made this. Oh well, I needed a break from work anyway. And Dad's band is making the whole house shake." She sets down the plate of nachos and sits in the beanbag next to Chelsea. I still have my arms raised. "So what are you kids doing? Wait, is that my easel?" She inspects me more closely. "Are you tired, sweetie?"

Caught. I drop my arms. "I'm fine. We're just playing."

"With my easel? Are you kids playing office?" She nudges Chelsea with her elbow. "I hope you demanded equal pay!"

Chelsea laughs. "No, Mrs. Kapoor, we're like four years too old to play office. Rahul was just telling me about this planning committee he wants to form."

"A planning committee?" Mom asks. "For what?" But, luckily, before I have to answer, she throws both her hands in the air. "Oh! Speaking of planning committees, I almost forgot. Rahul, did you tell Chelsea about the International Bazaar?"

"Tell her what about it?"

She looks at Chelsea. "We're getting a head start this year. So that we have plenty of time to build up a *huge* audience. With everything that's going on in the world, we really want the Bazaar to bring people together. To promote cultural understanding.

"So listen." She clasps her palms together. "Mona Auntie is heading the entertainment committee, and she has convinced all the aunties to be in an Indian dance. Can you imagine me dancing?" She wiggles her shoulders up and down and chuckles to herself. I make eye contact with Chelsea and roll my eyes. "But it's important to us that you kids participate, too. After all, you are the future. So, what do you think? Is there something you might want to do?" Then she makes her voice all singsongy. "You could join us in *our* dance"—she looks at us eagerly—"or you could do something on your own? Maybe the two of you?"

I almost choke trying not to laugh. There's no way we'd ever do a performance at the *Biz*arre. Most years, Chelsea and I sit in the back and make fun of the, like, three people who dare to get up onstage.

"Come on, kids. I promise it'll be fun. And I think the Bazaar can make a real impact this year."

I try to catch Chelsea's eye again, but she seems lost in thought.

Then she asks, “What kind of Indian dance are you guys doing?”

“We haven’t decided yet,” Mom answers. “It’ll be fun, though. Maybe Bollywood. Rahul, you love Bollywood movies. This would be perfect for you!”

“We’ll think about it, okay, Mom?” I gesture toward the stairs. “Now can Chelsea and I have some alone time? Before she has to go home?”

“All right, I’m going.” She tries to ruffle my hair, but I duck out of the way. “I know when I’m not wanted. But think about it.”

“Bye, Mom.” I wave as she heads up the stairs and shuts the door.

I turn to Chelsea. “I can’t believe my mom’s going to perform at the Bizarre. Remember when that woman from Thailand was dancing last year, and her pants ripped right down the back?”

Chelsea claps her hand to her mouth. “Oh my God. YES! And she had to finish the dance trying to cover her butt the whole time?!”

We both bust up so hard we’re doubled over.

She finally catches her breath and reaches for a nacho. “Anyway, what were we talking about?”

“My planning committee.” I pick up a marker.

“Right.” She crunches down on the chip. “What

is this all about anyway? Why are you so obsessed with this all of the sudden?"

"I don't know. No real reason. But do you have any ideas about what I could do?"

"Oh wait, I know!" she says, her mouth still full. "Why don't you join the Mathletes?"

I'm horrified. "THE MATHLETES?! Are you kidding, Chels? There's no way I'm joining the Mathletes!"

"Um, okay." She swallows. "Ra, you got a perfect score on your summer math homework. You're *good* at math. Why *wouldn't* you want to do it?"

"Um, because it's nerd central!" I argue. "It's kids like Jenny and Gina! And I already I told you I need something surprising. Besides, can you imagine what Brent would say? He already informed me all 'my people' are good at math!"

"Wait, *what*?" She squints her eyes. "Is this about Brent?"

Oh no. Shoot. Why did I say that?

"No! Forget I said that. NO! This is . . . This is just for *me*. I just want to do something, but it can't be, you know, nerdy or anything."

"Ra, we *are* nerds!" Chelsea says. "That's what makes us fun!" Then she looks down and fiddles with the cuff of her sock. "And, I mean, David said he might join."

I raise my eyebrows at her. "He did? When did he tell you that?"

"On Friday. When we were talking."

"Oh *really*? Interesting. What else did you talk about?"

"What does that mean? Nothing!" Chelsea says, little pink splotches forming on her cheeks. "Anyway, my point is, if you want to be the best at something, you should do that!"

I raspberry my lips and hang my head.

"Fine, I'll think about it," I say.

But there's no way I'm doing the Mathletes. I'll have to find something else on my own.

CHAPTER 10

Monday morning, in first period English, Mrs. Collins gives us a pop quiz. Her infamous first quiz of the year. The one every eighth grader at Greenville Junior High has warned every seventh grader about since the beginning of time.

I'm proofreading my answer to the last essay question right as the bell goes off. I sigh and get up to turn it in, when Brent slams a crumpled piece of notebook paper down on my desk.

"Catch ya later," he says, walking away.

"You coming, Ra?" Chelsea calls.

I pocket the note and hand in my quiz.

It takes three whole periods, until lunch, for me

to finally have a moment alone to read it. And even that isn't easy. I make up an excuse to Chelsea about needing to grab something from my locker, and then I wait in the hallway until everyone else clears out.

I lean into my open locker, half hidden behind the door, and unfurl the note:

So, are you? Are you gay?

I freeze.

I read the note again. Then I rip it up, over and over and over, until a little pile of torn paper rests against the front edge of my locker.

I'm scooping it up to throw it in the trash can when I hear, "Oh, hey, Rahul," over my shoulder.

It's Justin.

I hurl the heap of ripped paper into my locker and slam it shut. I spin around and press my back up against the door as though the note might magically reassemble itself and force its way out if I let up.

"You okay?" he asks, peering at me curiously.

"Yup," I say, my lips barely opening.

A voice down the hall bellows, "Go long!"

Justin whirls around, launching himself two feet into the air. His arms extend overhead, and his shirt rises ever so slightly.

I squeeze my eyes shut.

When I open them, he's softly landing on the ground, holding a football.

"Ha! I didn't even have to move!" Justin gloats, tossing the ball from one hand to the next.

"Whatever, J. Nice catch." Brent saunters over.

I back myself up a little harder against the locker door.

"'Sup, Rahul-io." Brent sneers at me. "Why are you creeping around the halls? Shouldn't you be at lunch?"

"I was just leaving," I croak. "Chelsea's waiting for me in the cafeteria." But I don't move, terrified to let go of my locker door. "Why aren't you guys at lunch?"

"'Cause." Brent throws his arms across his chest like he's a rapper or something. "We had to toss around the ol' pigskin."

"But we gotta head that way, too." Justin nods toward the cafeteria. "Before we get in trouble."

"That's called a pigskin?" I ask, throwing up just a tiny bit in my mouth.

"Uh, duh." Brent beats his chest with both fists. Like he's a gorilla or something. "And we have to get every minute of practice in that we can." He grabs the ball from Justin. "First scrimmage is right around the corner."

"Well, good luck," I say.

"You playing any sports this year?" Justin asks me.

Brent snorts into his fist. "Rahul? Sports? You've seen him run, right?"

Brent flings his limbs every which way again, and my face reddens.

"Dude. Enough." Justin swats the football out of Brent's hands.

"Fine, fine." Brent bends over to retrieve it. "My bad. I mean, you could *definitely* play a sport." He leans his elbow up over my head and into the locker next to mine, so that my face is practically inside his armpit. "Actually, now that I think about it, you know what? They're having late tryouts for the football team soon. For people who couldn't make the summer training camp." He takes a step back and his mouth widens like he's just had the idea of the century. "Rahul! You should totally try out for football."

I let out a weak laugh. "I don't think so."

"All right already, we gotta get to lunch," Justin interrupts.

"Lunch, shmunch, fine." Brent nods. "Walk with us, Rahul."

The three of us head down the hall, and just as we get to the cafeteria, Brent throws an arm around my shoulder and whispers, “See you at tryouts. Unless, for some *secret* reason, it makes you uncomfortable to hang out with Justin.”

My voice catches in my throat. “Why would that make me uncomfortable?”

Brent raises an eyebrow. “Exactly.”

All during lunch, I can see Chelsea’s mouth moving while she talks to me, but my mind is fixated on Brent. I know I’m not cut out for football. At all. But I hate that he’s lording it over me. And I don’t want him to think I’m too *scared* to hang out with Justin.

I bite my fingernail.

I mean, is it so impossible that I could make the team . . . ? It’s not like it’s the NFL or anything. . . .

Plus, all I have to do is pass the tryout. Once I’m on the team, I’d have plenty of time to practice. To get better.

Everyone would be so surprised I’m doing this. I wonder if there’s even an award for most improved player?

I mean, if I practice really, really, really hard . . .

Nah, it’s too crazy.

CHAPTER 11

"Remind me why we're doing this again?" Chelsea's pacing back and forth a few feet in front of the wooden fence in our backyard.

"Just 'cause. Now go long!" I lob the football up in the air, but it falls with a thud before it makes it even halfway to Chelsea.

"Rahul, zero, Chelsea, one." Bhai scratches it on the mini chalkboard resting on his lap.

"That's not how the scoring works!" I call, running up the lawn to get the ball.

It's my first time, as Brent said, actually "tossing the ol' pigskin" with another person. The only reason saying that doesn't make me barf is that Google assured me that footballs aren't *actually* made of pigskin. And even though they used to be made of animal bladders (vomit!), that was like over a century ago.

Mine is made of rubber. Vulcanized rubber.

"So how *does* the scoring work?" Bhai asks, wiping the slate clean.

From the garage, a speaker feeds back, and Chelsea, Bhai, and I plug our ears. Dad, Vinay Uncle, and Jeet Uncle are at it again in the garage, and Mom and the Auntie Squad have taken over the house.

"It's like this," I answer him. "I'm pretty sure you get six points if you get a touchdown. But then you *could* get an extra point. Or if you're lucky, I think you can even get two. I mean, not lucky. You obviously have to do something. Honestly, it's pretty confusing.

"You know what?" I pick up the ball. Why on earth are they still made in this weird triangle shape anyway? It makes it so hard to get a good grip on it. "It doesn't matter. According to my book, what we're doing today wouldn't really qualify for scores anyhow."

After pleading with Mom to take me shopping for the football, I also begged her to take me to the bookstore to buy *Football for Dummies*. She wasn't a fan of the title ("Just because I'm buying this for you doesn't mean I'm condoning the use of the word *dummy*!"), but she was happy I was getting any book at all.

"If there's no score, what am I doing here?" Bhai asks.

"Actually, why are we doing this at all?" Chelsea interrupts.

Here it comes. All week long, in addition to scouring *Football for Dummies*, I've also been doing home workouts in the safety of my bedroom. I've curled cans of chickpeas so hard I made the veins in my arms pop out. And I didn't just do regular pushups: I also put my feet up on the bed and hung over the side of it. According to the YouTube videos I watched, decline pushups are the key to a "massive chest."

It's all been in preparation for my first day on the field, or in my case, the backyard.

But I haven't told Chelsea, or Bhai, or even Mom or Dad yet, that I'm trying out for the football team.

"Well." I smile, still struggling to keep the football from slipping out of my hands. "Guess who's trying out for the football team in a couple of weeks?"

No one moves for what feels like a good minute.

Then Chelsea busts a gut. "THE FOOTBALL TEAM?!"

"Stop that. It's not *funny*!" I jog back to my starting position.

"Wait, are you serious?" She widens her eyes. "Ra, you can't just try out for the football team! You have to be, like, an athlete. Plus didn't football practice start weeks before school started?"

"Well, for people who couldn't make the summer practice, they do another round of tryouts. It's in the school manual. And today's kind of like a scrimmage, Bhai," I say, trying to steer us back on track. "There are no scores, but there's still a referee. *That's* why you're here."

"Actually," Chelsea says evenly, "in a scrimmage, there are scores. They just don't count toward standings."

"Right, no standings." I must have read that wrong. "That's what I was saying."

I drop down into a lunge stretch.

"No. No, you weren't. You don't know anything about football. You can't just join the team. I'm serious. You could get hurt. Like, for real. You could get a concussion!"

"A *concussion*?" Bhai wheels in a little closer.

"Relax." I set my hand down on the ground so I don't tip over. "I doubt I'll get a concussion."

"Well, you could. You know you'll get tackled and stuff, right? I mean, it's how my dad tore his ACL!"

"Tore his *what*?" Bhai asks.

"Wait." I stand back up. "Your dad played football?"

"Yeah, in high school. Until he got injured."

I throw my arms in the air. "Now you tell me! He played high school football?! Will he help me?"

Chelsea walks across the backyard and picks up the football at my feet. "I can't believe you want to do this." She tosses the ball back and forth in her hands and sighs. After what feels like an eternity, she says, "Fine, I *guess* I can ask him." Then I see a little glint in her eye. "Want me to show you some of the things he's already taught me? Sometimes we play in the backyard."

"You do?" I'm skeptical.

"We sure do." I can hear the pride in her voice. "To begin with"—she shows me her grip on the ball—"*this* is how you hold it."

I have no idea what she's doing differently, but she makes it look *so* easy.

"Second of all"—she widens her stance and pulls

the ball back by her ear—"this is how you throw it."

The ball spirals over our lawn and lands a few feet in front of the fence, the tip of it kicking up a smidge of dirt and grass.

I fall to my knees and use my best ET voice. "Teach. Me."

Chelsea shakes her head, but then she smirks and ETs me back. "I'll. Be. Right. Here."

Bhai whistles and holds up his little chalkboard like an Olympic judge. "Great throw! Ten-point-oh for Chelsea!" he screams. She tosses her hair back like it's no big deal.

"Okay, Ra." She turns to me. "Why don't we start with catching? I'll throw, you catch."

"Starting over!" Bhai barks. "Chelsea, zero, Rahul, zero!"

The first ball comes barreling straight at my nose. "No, no, no, nooooooooo!" I screech and catapult myself out of its path.

"Chelsea, one, Rahul, zero!"

The second ball falls into my arms, but the shock of the contact makes it bounce around and slide out of my fingers.

"That's a fumble!" Chelsea yells.

"What?! I had it in my arms!"

"Tell it to the ref!"

"Chelsea, two, Rahul, zero!"

"Bhai, really?" I dig my heels into the grass. "I already told you! That's not how it works!"

"Come on, Ra, you can do this!" Chelsea tries to pump me up. "You have to be fearless! Like, imagine you're a rock star! Like this ball couldn't hurt you if it tried!"

The third throw sails across the yard, like a missile headed right toward my forehead. But I steel myself. I refuse to move. It's cruising so hard I think I hear the wind whistling around its edges. I grit my teeth. It's inches away now. Right at the last second, I leap up to catch it. "I'm a rock star!" I scream, squeezing my eyes shut. My arms grasp the air blindly. I feel rubber scrape against my forearms. Vulcanized rubber. I pull the ball into my chest. The force of it knocks me backward. Air blasts out of my lungs as I hit the ground. My glasses ricochet across my face.

BUT I HAVE IT! I'm actually holding the ball.

I hear a long, slow clap from the side of our house, and I creak my head over to look. Blades of grass press into my cheek.

It's Vinay Uncle. He's coming out of our sliding glass door, followed by Dad and Jeet Uncle.

"*Wah, wah.* Good catch." Vinay Uncle turns to Dad. "I didn't know Rahul played sports." His voice has the slightest edge of contempt in it. "Maybe my boys could teach him"—his belly shakes—"how to catch the ball with his eyes open!"

Vinay Uncle's twin sons, Vimal and Vipul, are high school sports zombies. Last time we had dinner at their house, Arun and I were forced to spend the whole night watching ESPN on the enormous TV in their basement. Each twin was sprawled out over an entire sofa, while Arun and I had to sit cross-legged on the floor, eye level with their gnarly toenails. Talking was not allowed. Only grunting.

"I thought it was a really nice catch, Rahul," Dad says. "Didn't you, Jeet?"

Jeet Uncle stares at his feet. "Yes. Yes, it was very nice."

"Dr. Kapoor, did you know Rahul's trying out for the football team?" Chelsea asks, and Vinay Uncle's belly shakes again.

"Rahul, uh." Dad throws a glance in Vinay Uncle's direction. "We all know you're *very* good at sports, but . . ." He crosses his arms and shakes his head. "No. No, you're not."

"Why not?" I prop myself up.

"Do you know what kind of spinal injuries you could sustain? Trauma to the brain?" He starts to raise his voice. "Spend one day in the emergency room with me, and you'll change your mind about willingly trying to break all your bones!"

"ALL your bones?!" Bhai throws his chalkboard to the ground.

"Relax, Anish." Vinay Uncle jumps in. "He's a boy. Boys *should* play football. Builds character. My sons play."

"He's younger than your sons!"

"So? We played sports when we were young."

"We played cricket! Cricket is a noncontact sport!"

Now Mom's coming out of the sliding glass door, with Nandita Auntie right behind her.

"Oh, Chelsea, you're here?" Nandita Auntie smiles. "You look more beautiful every time I see you." She sneaks a wink at me.

"What's all the shouting about?" Mom asks.

Chelsea waves. "Hi, Mrs. Kapoor. Hi, Nandita Auntie."

"Oh, I love that you call me that." Nandita Auntie clutches her chest. "I *am* your auntie. And maybe one day I'll be your *real* auntie."

"I'm sorry, what?" Chelsea asks.

Juhi Auntie squeezes through the door. She says in her whispery voice, “Hi, kids, how are—”

Vinay Uncle must not hear her. Or maybe he does hear her, and he just doesn’t care. Either way he wraps his arm around Dad’s shoulder and loudly pronounces again, “*Boys* should play football.”

“What’s that?” Mom bristles.

“I am telling Anish that he should support Rahul in trying out for the football team,” Vinay Uncle says.

“What do you mean, trying out for the football team?” Mom asks. Before anyone can answer she says, “No. No way, Rahul. It’s too dangerous. Besides, you don’t play football.”

“Who says?” I get up off the ground. “Plus, you already bought me the football. And the book.”

“I . . . what?” Mom shakes her head. “I thought that was just for fun.”

“You even signed the permission slip last night,” I point out. “Remember?”

“I did? Well, I wasn’t paying attention. I was working! Anish, can I get a little help, please?” Mom turns to Dad.

Dad’s opens his mouth, but before he can speak, Vinay Uncle claps him on the back. “It’ll be good for him.”

Dad looks at Mom helplessly. Mom shakes her head no.

And then to my surprise Dad turns his palms up and shrugs. "You know what? Maybe he should try out. He *wants* to. He's obviously practicing. And the school will make sure he's safe, right? It's fine, Rahul."

Vinay Uncle punches his fist into his hand. "Good man, Anish! Good man!"

Mom shoots Dad a dirty look and whirls around. The sliding door slams shut behind her.

CHAPTER 12

The door to the boys' locker room slowly creaks open as I tiptoe inside. It brushes the corner of my gym bag and falls into place behind me with a soft thud. I poke my head to the left and to the right. It's just me.

Perfect.

If there's one thing I've learned from PE class, it's that it's a good idea to get undressed *before* everyone else barrels into the locker room. I mean, who wants to strip down to their underwear in front of people you have to stand in the lunch line with two periods later?

I drop my duffel bag down on the bench in front of the lockers and change into my shorts, doing my best to let only the very tippy toes of my sock-clad feet touch the floor before sliding them back into the safety of my gym shoes. This place is like a breeding ground for any number of life-threatening diseases. I stuff my bag into a locker and arrange my clothes in a crumpled-up pile on the bench so it looks like I'm in the middle of changing. Then I head to the restroom to wait. Once everyone else gets here, I'll sneak back out and everyone will think I was just off peeing.

As I'm making my way to the bathroom, I hear water dripping in the shower area.

No one *ever* showers after PE, so I never pay attention to this part of the locker room. The shower area is just a little open square with two shower heads on each of the walls. They seem awfully close to each other, and there are no curtains or anything.

Do football players shower after practice?

I guess I thought it'd be just like PE. That I'd just shower at home.

What about at away games? Is showering *required*?

Someone's voice ricochets off the walls, and I freeze. "Wassup, dude? You ready to kill it?"

"Yeah, to kill yo face!" another voice responds. They burst out laughing.

Wow. That's aggressive. I don't recognize them.

They must be eighth graders.

I gingerly dart to the bathrooms and lock myself in a stall.

Their footsteps clomp toward the lockers, and then I hear, "Wait, whose stuff is this? Is somebody in here?"

"Helloooooooo? Ding-dong! Anyone home?" They snicker.

Do I answer? My jaw is frozen shut.

I pull my feet up onto the toilet rim. Then I make the mistake of peering down. I wish I could spray a family-sized container of hand sanitizer in there.

More voices bound into the locker room. More footsteps clomp toward the lockers. Then someone walks into the bathroom area. I try to make myself as still as possible. A pair of sneakers stops in front of the space under my stall door.

Please don't try to come in here.

I glance at the latch. Definitely locked.

The sneakers move a step closer, and I hold my breath.

Finally, they walk away.

"You gotta be kidding me," I hear from out by the lockers, and the voice is unmistakably Brent's. "He's really gonna do it."

"Who's really gonna do what?"

"This is Rahul's stuff, isn't it?" Brent asks.

"Who's Rahul?" someone asks.

"Rahul Kapoor?" Brent says. "The nerdy Indian kid?"

"You mean the tall dude with a caterpillar lip?" someone asks, making everyone laugh.

"Nah," Brent says. "That's the *other* nerdy Indian." More people laugh. "The tall dude's Jai. With the weird accent."

Jai Parikh is in the eighth grade, and he's a total nerd by any standards. His family moved here from India two years ago. Last summer he shot up, like, two feet and started growing this really stupid-looking mustache.

I hear the door between the locker room and the gym fly open, and Coach Martinez's voice booms, "Let's go, let's go, let's go. Why are you all standing around in your underwear? What is this, a pajama party?

"Now listen up, most of you can dress out in full gear today, but I need a couple volunteers to skip the pads and helmets. I've got a latecomer who wants try out for the team, and I'll need some of you to put him through the paces."

I swallow. Paces?

There's a bunch of grumbling and someone says, "No one ever does the second tryout. Is that even really allowed?"

"Don't worry," Brent says, and I can just imagine him holding my things up in disgust. "I guarantee this won't take very long."

"Great. So then you'll be our first volunteer," Coach says, slapping him on the back. "Thank you, Brent. Now who else?"

Brent moans.

Another voice says, "Aw, come on, Coach, do we have to? It'll ruin practice."

"Thank you, James, you're my second volunteer. Now, I just need one more."

It gets so quiet, I can hear my breath.

"I'm happy to wait all day," Coach says. "We could also cancel practice entirely, and I could just run you guys around the track for the entire two hours."

The silence seems to go on and on until finally a voice says, "I'll do it."

It's Justin.

My stomach flips.

It's now or never. I let out a slow breath and step

off the toilet. I walk out toward the lockers as casually as possible.

"Oh, hey." I wave as confidently as I can manage. "Who's ready to crush this thing?"

Except for the dreaded days when we have to run track, PE class is mostly in the gym. Chelsea and I came to homecoming last year, but we spent the entire game talking our heads off. During halftime, we disappeared behind the stands and choreographed dances to the pep band songs.

So I guess it should be no surprise, as I trudge out to the field, that it feels like I'm in a foreign country. The track arcs out to infinity, and the numbers painted on the grass get smaller and smaller as the field stretches out before me. The goalposts tower over my head like skyscrapers.

"Go, Ra, GO!" I spin around to see Chelsea and Mr. Wilson standing on the edge of the track.

I dart over to them. "You guys, I'm so nervous!" I admit.

"You'll do great." Mr. Wilson kneels down and puts an arm on my shoulder. "Just remember what I taught you. Catch the fat part of the ball, and then immediately tuck it away."

"Right, right." I nod. He taps his fist on mine.

Chelsea leans in to hug me, and behind her I see Brent's dad pacing in the bleachers.

A whistle pierces the air and Coach Martinez bellows, "Rahul! Let's go!"

"Kill it out there!" Chelsea whispers.

As I jog toward the rest of the team, I catch Brent staring at me. I tighten my arms against my side so they don't flail around.

"First drill," Coach Martinez says, whipping out his clipboard, "is testing your running abilities. You'll run a half mile around this track. No stopping allowed. Got it?"

I nod. "How far is half a mile?"

"Two laps around."

"Two *whole* laps?" I stare at the track. "Any way I could just do one?"

"No. Now, ready, get set . . . GO!"

I shove my glasses up onto my nose, and I take off.

But the track is *so* hard under my feet. My legs feel like concrete pillars, and I'm already breathing too fast.

"Pace yourself, Rahul!" Mr. Wilson screams from the stands.

I slow up a bit. But, wait, am I being timed? I forgot to ask. I look over my shoulder. Coach is barking at the rest of the team, and I can make out a stopwatch hanging from his neck, but there's no way I can see if it's on.

It doesn't matter. I'm coming past the goalpost on the other side of the field. I'm a quarter of the way done. My breathing levels off a bit.

I mutter to myself, "You got this!"

As I come around the other side of the track, I take in the field. Someone tosses a ball to Brent, and to my surprise, he actually misses it. He looks over to the stands, and when I follow his gaze, I see his dad shaking his head. Brent punches himself in the arm. Three times. Really hard.

I suck in some air. My legs are killing me, but I'm almost back to where I started: the first set of goalposts. The freshly painted, gleaming yellow base is so close now.

"One lap down. One to go, Rahul," Coach Martinez calls. "Keep on trucking!"

I want to ask if he's timing me, but forming words seems impossible. It's hard enough just to breathe. My shins feel like metal rods hammering into my knees.

"You can do it, Ra!" Chelsea jumps up and down as I pass by them. I grin at her, and when she fist-bumps the air, I feel a jolt of energy.

But it only lasts about three seconds. God, is this hard. My T-shirt is soaked in sweat now, and the weight of it is pulling my shoulders down. My throat is clenched shut and my lungs are desperately trying to get more air.

I make it to the second set of goalposts and look down the track. Could it possibly be getting longer? Is that a thing?

Pain is knitting itself into the side of my stomach, and a charley horse seizes the back of my right calf. I hop up and down to shake it off, but quickly stop when I notice a couple of guys laughing and pointing at me from the field.

"No breaks, Rahul!" Coach Martinez hollers. He pulls his stopwatch up in front of his face.

I set my foot back down and will it to move forward, but every muscle in my body wants to stop.

I squeeze my eyes shut for a second, and I picture Bhai in front of me, whipping his head around. Laughing the world's greatest laugh. I hear his voice. "It's just to Mr. McCarter's Jeep!"

I clench my jaw and pump my arms. I can do this. I *have* to do this.

The first set of goalposts is so far away that it looks like it's made out of toothpicks.

"Almost there!" Chelsea is yelling from the stands.

The toothpicks start turning into pencils. Yes! I'm getting closer.

I let out a ragged scream and hurl my body the last five feet. I see the white marker line on the track in front of the goalpost and I fling myself over it.

I did it!

I collapse into a little ball on the maroon track.

A big, warm hand clasps my back. "You okay, Rahul?" Coach Martinez crouches over me.

I smile up at him. "Yup." My breath is still choppy. "Is that it?"

He chuckles. "Not quite. You ready for round two?"

There's a round two?

There is.

And in round two the torture only increases.

"Push-ups!" Coach Martinez hollers. "Twenty push-ups!"

TWENTY?

That's thirteen more than I've ever done in my room.

I don't know if it's adrenaline, the fact that I weigh basically nothing, or if I'm actually on my way to building a massive chest, but the first eleven aren't that bad. On twelve and thirteen my arms start to quiver, and I have to clutch the grass with my fingertips to steady myself. By fourteen my knees try to buckle underneath me, like they have a mind of their own. Fifteen and sixteen, my shoulders start to shake. At seventeen, I bite my lip so hard I'm not sure if it's sweat or blood dripping down my chin. At eighteen I have to stop at the top to catch my breath. My whole body is turning to jelly. Nineteen I almost wipe out at the bottom, blades of grass brushing against the tip of my nose. I hear Chelsea and Mr. Wilson chanting, "Just one more, just one more!"

I muster up every ounce of energy I have, pushing my body up as hard as I can.

"Twenty!" Coach Martinez slams his hand onto the ground next to my face.

"Sweeeeeeet!" I scream, falling spread-eagle onto the grass. "Is that it? Did I make the team?"

But before Coach can answer, someone hollers, "Hey, what's this all about anyway?" I look over and see Brent's dad jogging up to us. "I thought this was supposed to be *practice*." He tips his chin up at

Coach Martinez. “Aren’t you supposed to be coaching these kids?” He shields his eyes with one hand. “Why on earth are you coddling some latecomer who can barely squeeze out a set of push-ups? First game’s right around the corner. I don’t want to see these boys fail.”

Coach Martinez keeps his focus on his clipboard. “First game is coming up, Dean, but school policy says we hold late tryouts for the team. Everyone gets a fair shot.”

“Yeah, but this kid’s in no shape to—”

“Dean.” Coach interrupts him. “There’ll be plenty of time for practice. I promise.”

I glance up at Brent, and he’s clenching his jaw, one eye on his dad. He raises his arm. “Hey, Coach! Should we put him through the paces now?”

“Well, at least that’d be something,” Mr. Mason grumbles, reluctantly walking away.

Coach offers me a hand. I squeeze it tight and hoist myself up onto my rubbery legs. He lowers his voice. “Listen, Rahul, you made it past round one, and you made it past round two, and that’s pretty good. But honestly, you just barely made it. The third round is actually playing some ball. Are you sure you want to go through with this?”

I wring a little sweat out from the bottom of my shirt, my hands still shaking.

"It's truly okay if you want to call it a day," Coach says.

"Is this the last round?" I ask, clutching my side.

"Yes, it is."

I set my jaw. "Then I'm doing it."

"All right, boys, listen up!" Coach calls. Justin, Brent, James, and I are standing in a diamond. "There's no tackling here, only touch. No teams, each man for his own. All I want you to do is throw and catch. Rahul, I'm watching not only for how you handle the ball, but how well you block, get yourself open, and communicate with the other players. All right? Let's go!"

As everyone starts to spread out, Justin pats me encouragingly on the back. I turn to look at him, but a football goes swishing by my head.

Brent jeers, "Heads up, sucka. Let's go!"

I run to the ball and pick it up. I concentrate hard on holding it just how Mr. Wilson taught me.

I pull it back by the side of my face.

Justin is jogging out on my left. I make eye contact with him. He nods. I nod back.

"Go long!" I scream as I catapult my arm forward.

The ball shoots straight up in the air.

Like, literally straight up in the air. Like a fountain. Everyone tilts their heads back to watch it. Then it comes barreling right back down toward my face.

"No, no, no, no, noooooo!" I scream and throw myself out of its way, covering the back of my head with my hands. When I open my eyes, somehow Brent has caught the ball.

"Atta boy!" I hear his dad call out. "Now can we just end this already?"

Next play, James has the ball. "Throw it to Rahul!" Coach Martinez calls. James nods my way, but suddenly Brent is standing in front of me. The back of his sweaty T-shirt blocks my face.

"How can I? He's not getting open!" James complains.

"Rahul, you have to get yourself open!" Coach barks, both his hands on his knees.

I manage to tiptoe out from behind Brent, and as soon as my face clears his back, James aims the ball my way.

"I got it!" I shout.

Except I don't. It flies right through my hands.

Coach comes running in. "Rahul, listen, I'll give you one more shot, but if you miss the ball again, I gotta shut this down, okay?"

"Okay." I nod, but I can't let him shut this down. Not when I've gotten this far.

I look over at the stands and see Chelsea, both her fists pumping the air.

"I'm a rock star," I whisper to myself. "I'm. A. Rock. Star."

Justin has the ball now. James is blocking him from the front, so Justin backs up a little farther. I cut across the field, a fire raging in my calves as I turn to run. Brent's coming in my way, so I pick up the pace, ignoring the stitch in my waist.

Even though Justin is far down the field now, somehow it's like I see his face in close-up. His nostrils expand, and a bead of sweat trickles down the side of his nose. His eyelids drop down in slow motion, and I nod. "Ready," I whisper.

And then he hurls the ball across the field. It's flying so fast that every nerve in my body wants to run screaming. But instead, I dig my heels into the ground. The ball comes closer and closer and closer. I bare my teeth and bound up into the air. The football is inches away from me now. Oh my God, I'm going to get it. I'm actually going to get it. Fake pigskin brushes against my fingertips. I have it, I have it, I actually—

The next thing I know, my mouth is full of grass and the arm of my glasses is pressing into my cheekbone. I see a blurry football bouncing up and down like three feet away from me.

"Ow, ow, ow, ow, ow!" I moan. It feels like someone is jabbing a machete into my ankle. I reach my arm out, but the ball is too far away. "Did I catch it?" I ask. "I mean, before I dropped it. Did I CATCH it?"

Suddenly, Coach Martinez is kneeling over me. His face is as white as a sheet. "Rahul, are you okay?"

More knife-stabs up my leg.

"I'm fine!" I practically shout even though tears are now streaming out of my eyes. "What happened? Did I catch it? Did I make the team?"

CHAPTER 13

In retrospect, the ambulance was probably overkill.

But Coach Martinez insisted. "It could be broken, Rahul! There's no *way* I'm letting you walk on it."

Chelsea and her dad tore across the field in a panic. But once Chelsea saw how freaked out I was, she swore that both my ankles looked "pretty much the same size" to her. Even though it was clear one was turning into a baby watermelon.

A couple feet away from me Brent kept jumping in the air, twisting his legs underneath himself, and then hurling his body onto the ground. He shouted over and over, "Did you guys see that? Classic!"

His dad finally told him to knock it off. I thought it was pretty nice of Mr. Mason to stand up for me. But then he grabbed the back of Brent's shirt. "If you injure yourself trying to show off, you're grounded for life!" he yelled.

"Ignore the both of them," Mr. Wilson said, shaking his head. "Like father, like son."

I died of embarrassment as the sirens roared toward the field.

On the upside, it *was* pretty fun to ride in the ambulance. Mr. Wilson followed us in his car, and Chelsea got to ride in back with me. The EMT even took a selfie with us. She was super nice when she realized I was Dr. Kapoor's son. She high-fived me and said, "Hey, don't be hard on yourself. When you're a football player, you're bound to get a few battle wounds, right? Way to take one for the team."

I didn't have the heart to tell her that I wasn't *on* the team.

I'd begged and begged Coach Martinez to give me one more shot. "Rahul," he'd said, one hand glued to his forehead. "You got injured during *tryouts*! There's no way you can be on the team. Have you seen your ankle?" Then he'd stopped himself. "Actually, my bad, don't look."

"Maybe don't look," Dad repeated, once we were in the emergency room. He slid his hand under my leg and tenderly prodded at my ankle.

"Ah, ha, ha, ha, ha," I moaned with each push.

"Oh boy." He sighed. "Guess this means I'm sleeping on the sofa. For the rest of my life."

"Why? Is it bad?" I propped my head up. My ankle was turning twenty shades of burgundy and blue.

"No, no, no, no, no." Dad wiped off the beads of sweat forming on his forehead. "It's probably nothing. But why don't we take an X-ray just to be sure?"

He turned back just before closing the curtain on the side of my hospital bed. "No more football for a while, okay, Rahul?"

The X-ray was quick, and now finally—with Dad off doing some work and Mr. Wilson looking for coffee—Chelsea and I get a minute alone.

"Can you believe this?" I ask, the medicine making the throbbing in my ankle slowly subside.

She squeezes my arm, standing next to the bed.

"I don't think you should make a habit of this, but," she says, smiling, "we did get some pretty sweet pics in the back of the ambulance."

I laugh. Then I force myself to look her straight in the eye. "Chels, honestly, tell me the truth. Did I catch the ball? Like at all? Like even for a second?"

"Ummm." She wrinkles her nose. "Debatable. But it doesn't matter, Ra. How long did you practice? Like, a few weeks? All things considered, you did pretty good out there. I didn't know you could do twenty push-ups!"

"Honestly?" I suppress a laugh. "I *can't*! I have no idea how that happened! That's the most I've ever done! In my life!"

"Um, it happened 'cause you're awesome!" she says.

We do a teensy BRiC.

"Anyway." She pulls up the chair next to the bed. "If you really want to play football, just keep training on your own and try out again next year, right?"

Next year? I think to myself. Next year is too far away. I can't wait that long.

Plus, do I really even *want* to play football?

A wave of embarrassment crashes over me again as I think about all the new fodder I've given Brent.

The curtain next to my bed flies open, and Mom's face pops in. Worry lines crease her forehead.

"Rahul, are you okay? I got here as fast as I could. What happened?"

Dad comes running up behind her before I can answer. "Nothing to be concerned about. I examined it myself, and I'm pretty sure it's fine. Let's not get upset."

"We'll know more when we get the X-ray," Chelsea pipes in.

Mom turns ever so slowly to Dad, her eyes flashing. "Did she say an X-ray?"

"Thank you, Chelsea." Dad smiles weakly. "But why don't you let me handle it from here?" He takes an almost imperceptible step backward. "I *did* order an X-ray, but just as a precaution. I'm 99 percent sure it's nothing. Just a minor injury."

"How minor?" Mom taps her foot. "And why aren't you 100 percent sure?"

"It's presenting like a *very* minor injury." Dad purses his lips and nods. "Probably just a sprain."

Mom guides Dad out with one hand on his back. With her free hand she slams the curtain behind her, making all the little curtain rings jangle up and down on the rod.

Their hushed conversation slips in through the cracks. "Anish, I told you he shouldn't try out! This is your fault."

"How is this my fault? Besides, he's a boy. These kinds of things happen to boys."

"To *boys*? Who's talking now? You or Vinay?"

"What's that supposed to mean?"

"You know what I mean!" Mom huffs. "Why do you care so much about what Vinay thinks in the first place?"

There's a pause. I lean in to try to hear what Dad's going to say. But before he can answer, Mr. Wilson's voice interrupts them, and then three sets of footsteps go walking away.

Chelsea pokes me in the arm. "Your dad is in *major* trouble." She snickers.

But I don't feel like laughing anymore.

She pulls her iPad out of her book bag and climbs up onto the edge of the bed. "Want to watch an episode of something while we wait for your X-ray results?"

"Sure." I nod.

She scrolls through her iPad.

And that's when it comes to me. An idea starts to blossom in my head. An idea free from the demands of athletic abilities.

"Something on Netflix?" she asks.

But now my brain is racing. "Acting," I whisper.

"What's that?" Chelsea looks up from the iPad.

"I could be an actor."

"Come again?" She sets the iPad down.

"You know. An actor. Like, a celebrity."

"You mean, like, be in the school musical again?"

Last year, Chelsea and I both tried out for the school musical. It was this really old-timey musical called *Brigadoon* that's set in Scotland. We rehearsed our songs over and over until they were basically perfect, so you can imagine our surprise when the cast list went up and we were both relegated to "townspeople." Even though Mrs. Daugherty, the drama teacher, said that the townspeople could only fake-talk during the group scenes, Chelsea insisted we learn actual Scottish accents to keep things authentic. We spent every performance trying to make each other crack up. We'd whisper things like, "Bonnie morn to you, lassie," and "Don't you be a wee scunner!" while doing townspeople chores.

"I don't mean the musical," I say. "I mean a *professional* actor. Like, someone famous."

"I'm not following."

I twist the sheet in my fist. "Like on TV."

"Um, okay." She picks the iPad back up. "I think those pain meds are going to your head. *How* are you going to be on TV?"

"What do you mean, how?"

"Rahul, we live in Indiana! Nobody in *Indiana* is on TV!"

She's got a point.

"It doesn't matter. I'll figure something out."

"Uh-huh," she says, and I hear the skepticism in her voice.

"I will, Chels!" I prop myself up, biting my tongue from the pain that shoots up my ankle. "But you have to help me. I mean, I could never have done football without you."

"I don't know how helpful I was," Chelsea says. "I mean, Ra, you just broke your ankle."

"No, I didn't. You heard my dad. It's probably just a sprain!"

As soon as I say it, Dad pushes his way through the curtains, staring at the folder in his hands with a look of triumph. "Sarita, come here!" he hollers.

"What is it?" Mom comes running in.

"I was right! It's just a sprain!" He pumps his fist

in the air. "Looks like someone's no longer sleeping on the sofa!"

"Sleeping on the . . . what?" Mom grabs the folder out of his hands.

"Never mind." Dad pats himself on the back. "Never you mind."

I smile at Chelsea. "See?"

CHAPTER 14

"Chelsea's here!" Bhai calls from upstairs.

"Can you ask her to come down?" I shout back from the basement, where I'm setting up for our photoshoot.

I wish we could hang out with Bhai today, but there's just too much to do.

I set a stool down onto the shag rug between the two standing lamps I've dragged over. I tilt both lampshades back until the light hits the stool just right. Then I bend over and mash the carpet down near the base of each lamp. Hard. I don't want any pesky rug hairs to make their way into that little hole where the electrical cord goes into the lamp base. The last thing

I need is to set the whole basement on fire.

I look over at the coffee table. Dad's camera. Check. Three telephoto lenses. Check. Detachable flash. Check.

Then I step back to admire my handiwork, careful not to put too much pressure on my ankle.

When we finally left the hospital, Dad told me I was extremely lucky. That my mild sprain would only need a few weeks of rest, ice, compression, and elevation. "Just have to RICE it!" he said as he bandaged my ankle. "And a little physical therapy." Then he raised his voice sternly so Mom could hear him. "And like I already told you, no sports for a while."

He didn't have to say it twice.

Staying off my foot has given me the perfect excuse to hole myself up in my room scouring the internet for professional acting opportunities. Chelsea was right though—so far I haven't found anything TV-related in the entire state of Indiana. Like, zilch.

Just multiple websites on things every actor needs to know so they're ready for that magical moment when "opportunity meets preparation!"

And one of those is "A perfect headshot can land you the job!"

"Rahul, you're never going to guess what I found!"

Chelsea comes bounding down the stairs. She peels off her denim jacket to reveal an "Arms Are for Hugging, Not for Fighting" T-shirt. Then she reaches into her back pocket and pulls out a folded-up, glossy one-page newsletter. She thrusts it into my hands.

"'Greenville People's Bank Offers No-Fee Checking Accounts'?" I read the title out loud. "Well, look at that!" I try to sound enthusiastic. "Were the fees, like, really high before?"

"No! Ra!" She grabs the newsletter out of my hands and flips it over. "Look! Right here."

There on the way bottom of this glossy piece of paper, next to where Chelsea's half-chewed, painted-blue fingernail is pointing, in a font so small I have to squint to read it, it says:

> *Greenville People's Bank will be casting a ten-to-thirteen-year-old boy for a local television commercial advertising our new no-fee checking accounts. Open auditions will be held on Friday, October 6, from four to six p.m., on a first-come, first-serve basis. Please bring a headshot. Nonunion job. No preparation necessary.*

"Oh my God!" I scream. "I'm ten to thirteen! I'm nonunion! This is it! This is the thing we've been waiting for!"

Now Chelsea's screaming in my face, too. "I know! That's why I'm showing it to you!"

"And we're about to take my headshots anyway!"

"I know!" Chelsea screams again. "It's perfect!"

We both finally calm down for a second, catching our breaths.

"This is gonna be great, Ra! And I've already come up with a pitch for your audition."

"Really? What's the pitch?"

"You're the ideal spokesperson for a bank because you're so good at numbers!"

What?

"Well." I nod. "We'll have to work on that. But I can't believe you found this! It's like a sign!" I throw my arms around her. "Thank you!"

"Okay, okay." Chelsea gently extricates herself from me. "They still have to cast you."

"Right! Oh my gosh, there's so much to do." I start rolling my head around in large circles and sticking my tongue in and out of my mouth. I stretch my cheeks up and down. "Blaaaaah, blaaaaaah, blaaaaaah." I yawn.

"Ra, this isn't the school musical. You don't have to, like, warm up to sing."

"I know." I grab her arm. "But I've been doing

this every day. Remember how we'd laugh at all of Mrs. Daugherty's relaxation exercises? Well, it turns out she knew what she was talking about!" I raise my eyebrows and smoosh them back down over and over again. "I read all about it online." I stretch my arms out and start spinning them around. "The number-one key to good acting is being *very* relaxed. The most famous acting teacher in the world, Stanislavski, said that being tense is the actor's greatest enemy."

I hobble over to the stool.

"Okay," Chelsea says. She starts rolling her shoulders around, too. "I'm *soooo* relaxed," she says. She sticks her tongue in and out of her mouth back at me. "Blaah, blaah, blaah!"

Now her eyes are bugging out, and we both start laughing. "Stop!" I cry, clutching my side.

"Now can we do something that's actually important?" She picks up Dad's camera. "Like take some headshots?"

"Wait, before we take the pictures"—I hop up onto the stool —"what do you think the commercial will be about?" I pull off my glasses and angle my head into the light. "Like, what should I try to look like?"

"I dunno. It doesn't say. It just says no preparation necessary. So I guess you should just be yourself."

"Are you sure?" I ask.

She pushes the button and the camera *click-click-clicks*, taking a series of pictures.

"Aw," she says, pouting her lips at the screen on the back of the camera. "These are *so* good!"

"Let me see!"

"You probably don't need all these lamps. The lighting could use some work. But I think you'll be pleased."

She hands me the camera.

Oh no. I'm not pleased. I'm *definitely* not pleased.

My eyes look all weird to me without my glasses on. My skin is swimming in a sea of grease, my nose takes up half my face, and the flash bouncing off my braces makes it look like a shooting star just flew out of my mouth. Also, my arms look like two brown toothpicks jabbed into the short sleeves of my polo shirt.

"Cute, right?" Chelsea smiles expectantly.

"No." I feel the panic rising up into my throat. "Not cute. Not cute at all!"

I shove the camera back into her hands and run over to the stack of clothes draped across the sofa. I definitely need to put on a long-sleeve shirt.

"We need to get a towel to wipe down whatever's

happening with my face," I say, wriggling out of my polo, "and I definitely can't smile with my mouth open! Is there an angle that will make my nose disappear? Is that something you can fix with lighting?"

"Ra, relax. These photos are adorable. They look just like you."

"They do?" I cringe, sliding my arm into a dress shirt. That's not at all what I wanted to hear.

"I think they really capture your personality. Look at the excitement in your eyes."

The door to the basement squeaks open, and Arun comes scurrying down the stairs.

"What are you guys doing?" Arun asks.

"Not now! Get out!" I go to chase him out, my shirt still half unbuttoned.

But now he's screaming up the staircase. "Mom! Rahul has his clothes off, and Chelsea's taking pictures of him!"

"Arun, stop that!" I say. "He's lying, Mom!"

Too late. Mom starts making her way down.

She warily eyes my clothes strewn out on the sofa. "You know I totally trust you, but what exactly are you two doing down here? Why is your shirt unbuttoned, Rahul? And does Dad know you're using his expensive camera? That's not a toy, you know."

"He was just changing outfits." Chelsea scrolls through some of the pictures, showing the camera to Mom. "We're taking headshots. Rahul's auditioning for a Greenville People's Bank commercial next Friday."

"What commercial?" Mom asks.

"This." I hand her the flyer.

"You're going to be on TV?" Arun asks incredulously. Mom's eyes dart back and forth across the paper.

"Yes, Arun," I sigh. "I mean, I have to audition, but yes."

"Well, this is wonderful." Mom looks up. "Are you auditioning, too, Chelsea?"

"No. Big surprise, they want a *boy*." Chelsea nods knowingly at Mom.

"Go figure." Mom rolls her eyes. "Well, it's nice you're helping Rahul. And doing something artistic. Is there anything I can do?" But then she shakes her head. "Oh, wait. Speaking of artistic. Have the two of you put any more thought into the Bazaar? Mona Auntie keeps bugging me to ask you."

"Yeah. We're not gonna do it," I say.

"Wait." Chelsea bites her lower lip.

"Yes, Chelsea?" Mom watches her.

Chelsea wriggles her toes on the shag rug. "I *might* want to do something. But I haven't really thought about, like, *what* yet."

My jaw drops. What is she talking about?

"Fantastic!" Mom says. "And it's okay if you don't have it all figured out just yet. Take your time. But I'm telling Mona Auntie you're in." Then she waggles her eyebrows. "I told you before, but if you think you can keep up with me and the aunties, you could be in our Bollywood dance."

Chelsea holds back a laugh. "Maybe."

Mom turns to me. "Does this make you change your mind, Rahul?"

Before I can answer, Arun starts screaming, "I'm ready for my headshot! Who's gonna take my picture?"

We all turn to see him sitting on the stool.

With his shirt off.

"Oh boy." Mom takes Arun's hand and grabs his T-shirt. "All right, we'll let you guys finish. Arun. Upstairs. Now. Chelsea, I'll give Mona Auntie your dad's number. Now try to convince Rahul. And Rahul, I think it's great you're auditioning for this commercial." She ruffles my hair. "In fact, I'm going to stop working early next Friday and take you to the audition myself."

As they head up the stairs, I hear Mom say, "Arun, not the pants. Please keep the pants on."

When they're gone, I turn to Chelsea. "Wait, what's this about? You want to be in the Bizarre now?"

"Yeah." She raises a shoulder. "I mean, I thought more about it, and why not?"

"*When* did you think about it? How come I didn't know?"

She ignores me. "Ra, we both love to dance. And it's for a good cause. All that stuff your mom said about culture, bringing people together. I mean, I hadn't really thought of it that way before. Don't you want to be a part of that?"

"Bringing people together? No one ever even goes! I only go because my parents *make* me. And because you and your dad come."

As soon as I say it, I get why Chelsea wants to do this. I mean, her dad took her to a bluegrass concert this summer to promote world peace. They had to camp in a tent and bathe in a creek.

I smile at her "Arms Are for Hugging" T-shirt. "Chels, I have a feeling it's just gonna be the same old Bizarre it always is. Now, can we take some more pictures?"

That night I have the best dream. I'm watching myself in the commercial for the Greenville People's Bank. As it starts, I'm outside on a big green lawn, playing football. The ball flies into the corner of the TV screen and I jump up and catch it perfectly. My feet hit the ground ever so smoothly and my biceps bulge as I bring the ball in to my chest. When I smile at the camera, my braces are gone and my teeth gleam white. My hair sweeps gently across my face, and I brush away my bangs. I say, "I keep my entire allowance at Greenville People's Bank. After all, who else has no-fee checking accounts?"

Later, I pull up in a limousine to school. My driver lets me out of the back door and a couple of the girls in my grade get so giggly, they have to run away. I shake my head: don't they know I'm still just a normal kid? Justin walks over, and he looks super nervous. "Hey, Rahul. I had no idea you were such a good actor. You should have been the lead in *Brigadoon*!" I open my mouth to answer him but my phone buzzes.

"Sorry, Justin, this is probably my agent," I say, when a commotion breaks out behind me. It's Brent trying to sneak a selfie, but Chelsea cuts him off. "No pictures, Brent. If I've told you once, I've told you a million times, you have to go through his publicist. Now, am I going to have to call his bodyguards? AGAIN?" Brent's face turns bright red. And then a rainstorm of flashbulbs goes off. I shield my eyes.

The paparazzi are relentless.

CHAPTER 15

"Finish the last bite, Arun. Come on, I thought you liked pancakes." Mom's loading the last of the breakfast plates into the dishwasher.

"I do like them, it's just too early for my stomach."

I look over at him. He's twirling his fork in a puddle of maple syrup on his plate.

"Arun, you better not make us late today. Hurry up!" I tuck my undershirt into my slacks and peer over Bhai's shoulder. He's ironing one of my dress shirts on the wheelchair-accessible ironing board that folds out of our kitchen cabinet. "Are you using the steam setting?" I ask. I reach for the can of starch next to him and start spraying the sleeve.

Bhai grabs the can out of my hands. "Stop micromanaging. You're acting like your mom."

"I'm not a micromanager." Mom laughs. "I'm just the smartest one here, so I have to tell everyone else what to do."

"Okay, ha, ha, ha. Can everybody just please focus?" I'm so nervous. Today is the day of the audition, and I feel like my insides are going to splatter all over the kitchen. I've felt this way ever since my alarm went off this morning. I've stuck my tongue in and out of my mouth and stretched my face a million times, but I'm still so tense.

Mom snatches up Arun's plate and scrapes the one uneaten pancake bite into the sink. "Relax, Rahul. Arun, come on, let's get in the car. Rahul, put your shirt on. We'll be waiting for you outside."

Bhai hands me the dress shirt, and I carefully slide my arms into the sleeves.

"Wait? Is this just going to get all wrinkly again at school? Why didn't I think of that before?"

"Rahul." Bhai looks straight into my eyes. "Just don't bend your arms at school." He suppresses a smile. "At all. Not even a little bit. Then you'll be fine." Bhai flips the ironing board back into the cabinet and wheels himself out.

"Yeah, right. Very funny," I call after him.

Outside, Mom honks the horn, and for a second I contemplate running upstairs to grab a different shirt. But instead I find myself staring at the plug hanging out of the iron. Panic floods my stomach. What if Bhai had accidentally left it plugged in? Could it have started a fire while we were out? "Definitely unplugged," I say to myself. I lightly skim my fingers along the five dials of the stove, where Mom was making us pancakes. "Off, off, off, off, off," I whisper. "Definitely off."

Mom honks the horn again.

I walk as fast as I can. Well, as fast as I can while moving my arms like a robot.

I pull the front door shut behind me. Then I turn so Mom and Arun can't see what I'm doing, and I grab the doorknob. I push and pull the door five times. "Definitely locked."

The school day feels interminable, but somehow, at last I'm sitting in Mr. Hayden's class. The last class of the day.

I stare at the minute hand on the clock as he

reads the question he's scrawled on the whiteboard out loud.

"Okay, everyone. Three parts to this quiz, so pay attention: If Trolley A leaves at nine a.m. for Nowheresville and Trolley B leaves at ten a.m. for Podunkville, I want to know, one, what time will they cross paths, two, what time will A get to Nowheresville, and three, what time will B get to Podunkville? Time starts now!"

We're already in Podunkville, I think. But it doesn't matter. Ten more minutes and it will finally be three thirty. The school bell will ring, and my life will change forever.

I flip open my notebook, but my eyes drift back to the clock.

The minute hand hovers and hovers and hovers until it finally *cha-chunks* down a notch. Nine more minutes.

Across the aisle, Justin is frozen, staring at his blank notebook, biting the end of his eraser. In front of me, the back of Brent's head moves from side to side like he's still reading the question on the whiteboard.

I pick up my pencil.

Shoot. My hand is shaking.

How is it possible to *still* be this nervous? I've felt this way for over eight hours now.

What did Stanislavski say about being tense?

I close my eyes. I concentrate on slowing my breath down. I try to picture what the audition will be like. How many people will be there? What will they make me do?

I peek over at Chelsea, but she's writing in her notebook. I wish she'd look up at me.

I unzip my backpack and try to peer at the bank flyer without anyone seeing me. Did it really say don't prepare *anything*? How is that possible?

"Rahul." Mr. Hayden's voice is in my ear. I swing forward and grab my pencil. I squeeze it hard to keep my hand from shaking. "There are only two minutes left." He kneels next to my desk. "Are you having some trouble with this one?" He looks concerned. "Did you know you're sweating? A lot?"

"I am?" I finger my collar. Oh no! Have I sweat-stained my shirt?

"Do you need more time?" Mr. Hayden asks.

I glance at the clock, the minute hand threatening to fall on the half-hour mark any second now.

"No. No, I can do this." I bite my lower lip and start scratching in the formulas. My handwriting is a little shaky, but my brain seems intact. I jot down the final answers: 1) 11:30 a.m., 2) 12:30 p.m., and 3) 1:15 p.m.

"Wow. Nice work." Mr. Hayden smiles as I tear the paper out of my notebook.

The bell goes off, and I chuck my math book into my bag.

Chelsea can't meet me at my locker fast enough.

"Help!" I beg.

"Help what? Are you ready to go?"

"Ready to go? NO! It's over!"

"What's over? What do you mean?"

"Look at me," I moan. "I'm a mess! Do I have sweat stains on my neck?"

"Rahul, stop it. You look great."

"No, I don't!" I throw my hands up in the air, nearly knocking Krista Mitchell in the face as she walks by us.

"Oops. Sorry about that." I smile, lowering my voice to keep from attracting any more attention. Clumps of students file out toward the parking lot.

"Chelsea." I hang my head. "I'm a sweaty mess." I unzip my book bag and carefully pull out the headshot

I printed on our color laser printer last night. "I look nothing like this."

Chelsea's mouth forms an O, but no sound comes out. I turn the photograph over and look at it myself.

I let out an involuntary gasp.

Chelsea had warned me, but I wanted the picture to be, well, picture-perfect. So, I did just the teensiest bit of editing to it . . . just a little.

So *why* do I look like an alien?

My skin is so light it looks like a beige paint sample, my eyes are so big they look like they belong on a cartoon, and my nose is so small it's like I just have two holes in the middle of my face.

I fling my locker door open and inspect my reflection in the magnetic mirror hanging inside. My sweaty skin, glasses, and braces stare back at me.

"I can't win!" I fling the door shut.

I glance down the hall, which is quickly emptying out, and turn to Chelsea.

"I can't go like *this*"—I point at myself— "and I certainly can't go like *this*!" I wave the headshot in the air.

"Okay." Chelsea takes a breath and tugs on the straps of her backpack. "Don't worry about the picture." Her voice is all business. "You'll be there in person, so forget about the headshot. Now, as for you . . ." She sizes me up. "It's gonna be fine! I thought ahead." She digs into her book bag and pulls out a powder compact. Then she whispers conspiratorially, "I brought some makeup."

"Makeup?" I whisper back, lowering the compact with my hand. I look up and down the hall. "Why do you have this?"

"My cousin left it at our house last Thanksgiving."

"Thanksgiving? That was almost a year ago! Is it still good?" I picture my face breaking out into a million zits.

"Rahul, we're running out of time. Don't overthink this."

"Fine," I concede. "Let's do it. But not here. I don't want anyone to see. Boys' bathroom?"

I stealthily drag Chelsea down the hall. But just as I'm about to push the door to the boys' room open, David walks out.

He stops, blocking the door. "Oh, hey, Rahul. Hi, Chelsea."

We stand frozen in front of him.

"Are you guys trying to get in here?" he asks.

Chelsea blushes. "What? *Me*? In the boys' room? Ha. HA! No."

But we still don't move.

David tries to maneuver around us. "Okay. Well, then I guess I'll let you guys *not* go into the boys' room."

He brushes past us, and then calls over his shoulder as he walks away, "Bye, Chelsea."

She drops her face into both of her palms.

"Come on! We have to hurry!" I say.

I dart into the bathroom first and make a quick sweep under all the stall doors. The coast is clear. I pull Chelsea in.

Her immediate reaction to the row of pee-stained urinals, crumpled paper towels spilling out over the trash bin, and faint stench of farts is enough to tell me that the girls' room is nothing like the boys' room.

"Ew! Ew! Ew!" She flutters her hands up and down like they're covered in slime. "How do boys live like this? Do you guys just pee standing right next to each other, right out in the open?"

I look at the urinals, which have no dividers between them.

"Not on my life! I use the stalls!" I say. "Let's do

this. Mom's probably had to circle the parking lot three times by now. And someone could come in any minute."

Chelsea pulls out the compact. She leans in and pats the powder-filled puff all over my face.

I look in the mirror. I'm white as a ghost.

"Oh shoot." She bites her bottom lip. "That was not the right skin tone at all. I forgot my cousin's white." She delicately grabs a paper towel, using just the tips of her fingers, and starts toward me.

"No, wait." I'm fixated on my reflection. It's a little garish, but I also kinda like how light it makes my skin look. "This could be good."

Chelsea arches her eyebrows. "I don't think so, Ra. I think I put too much on."

Just then the bathroom door flies open, and we both freeze.

No, no, no, no, no.

It's Brent.

"Aw, man!" he roars, staring at the compact in Chelsea's hand. "This is too good! What in the heck are you guys doing?"

"We were just . . ." Chelsea goes to answer, but now Brent is doubled over in laughter.

"Are you doing Rahul's makeup?" He bangs his

fist on the counter. “I hate to break it to you, makeup or no, you’ve got a face even yo momma wouldn’t want to kiss.”

I steel myself. “That is not true, Brent. My mom kisses me all the time.”

“Oh, Ra . . .” Chelsea puts her hand over her face.

“OH MY GOD!” Brent flings the door open and yells out to the hallway, “HE JUST ADMITTED IT! RAHUL KAPOOR MAKES OUT WITH HIS MOM!” Then he slams the door shut behind him.

I stand there, frozen for a second. Then I force myself to put Brent’s voice out of my head. “Come on! We have to go!”

CHAPTER 16

Chelsea and I race to the parking lot and jump into the back row of Mom's minivan.

"Where have you two been?" Mom flicks on the turn signal and starts pulling out. "The entire school already left. I had to pick up Arun and come back, you took so long!"

Arun is sprawled out across the entire row of seats in front of us, and to my surprise, Bhai is in the front passenger seat.

"*You're* here, Bhai?"

"Of course! Did you think I would miss your first step to becoming a movie star?" He chortles out one of his infectious laughs. "And I brought you a freshly ironed shirt!"

"You *did*?" I'm so happy I almost forget about Brent. Bhai passes the shirt back to me.

Arun sticks his nose between the headrests and stares at me.

"What do you want?" I ask, as icily as possible.

"Why does your face look like that?"

"It's just a little makeup."

"You're wearing MAKEUP?!"

Mom shoots a questioning glance our way in the rearview mirror.

"All actors do, Rooney," Chelsea butts in. "Haven't you ever watched TV?"

Arun's eyes dart back and forth between us, like we're trying to dupe him or something. "Okaaay. But why is it so white? You look like a clown."

"Turn around and mind your own business," I say.

Mom turns into the Greenville People's Bank parking lot, but a sea of minivans and station wagons is already occupying every available space. She pulls out and glides into an opening along the curb.

Through the window, I see other boys my age

heading toward the front entrance of the bank. Each with a parent in tow. Or at most two parents. I count all the heads in our car. There are *five* of us.

"Maybe some of you should wait outside." I try to hide the anxiety in my voice.

"No way! We're all coming with you!" Bhai opens his car door.

Ugh. Why do there always have to be, like, twenty people wherever we go? Even when Mom and Dad surprise us with a trip to Pizza Hut, the entire Auntie Squad and Uncle Brigade always have to tag along, taking over the entire restaurant and ruining a night of perfectly good pizza.

I resignedly duck behind the seat to change button-downs. Chelsea and Arun let themselves out of the side of the van, while Mom opens the trunk to get Bhai's wheelchair.

"Rahul," Mom calls, "come help me."

I meet Mom at the back of the van, and she studies my face. "Are you trying to make your skin lighter?" she asks. "Where did you get that powder?"

"What? No," I say, feeling embarrassed. "Chelsea brought it. Because I was sweating."

I see the concern in Mom's face, but she says, "Okay," and then closes the trunk.

I hold the wheelchair steady as Bhai lowers himself in. A kid and his dad walk by us.

"Good luck, little man!" Bhai calls, waving at them.

"Don't be nice to them! They're the competition!" I whisper-shout. "And try not to be so loud. This is a bank, not our backyard."

Mom pulls Bhai's hat down snug around his ears. "Rahul, I know you're nervous, but don't be disrespectful."

"I'm not nervous! And I wasn't being—"

"Are you warm enough, Bhai?" Mom cuts me off.

I feel a tinge of guilt as I realize just how cold it must be out here for him. Fall has definitely taken over. Red and yellow leaves have gathered in little piles along the curb, and the grass is turning brown. And even though it's only four p.m., the sky is a dark, dark gray.

"I'm sorry, Bhai." I put a hand on his shoulder. "Want me to push you?"

"*Push* me?" He laughs, and I can tell he's already forgiven me. He bears down on his wheels and leads our motley crew up the bank parking lot.

Chelsea falls into step with me as Mom zips up Arun's windbreaker. My mouth suddenly goes dry, making it hard to swallow, and when I look down, my fingers are trembling ever so slightly. I quickly stuff my whole hand into my pocket.

"Did you lock the van, Mom?" I turn back to ask.

"I think so, but I'm not too worried about it in any case."

"Should we just check anyway?"

She sighs and fumbles around in her purse. I hear the *beep-beep* of the automatic locks and finally manage to swallow some of my own saliva.

I've been to Greenville People's Bank a million times with Mom. Sometimes we just use the ATM outside. Once we went to the room where they bring out your safe-deposit box, and Arun and I got to check out all of the Indian jewelry Mom wore to her wedding but no longer has any use for. Everyone always smiles at us, and Arun and I walk away with an insane loot of lollipops.

But today, as Bhai glides up the wheelchair ramp to the main entrance, I feel a sense of dread. The tip of my shoe snags on the top stair, and I almost fall flat onto my face.

"Easy, Rahul," Mom says. "Your ankle is just getting better. You have to be careful."

"I know." I nod.

The glass doors waft open in front of us, and the "Caution Automatic Door" sign flashes a bright-yellow warning.

Chelsea lightly punches me in the shoulder. "You ready to kill it, Ra?"

I try to smile back at her, but it feels like my right eye is on my left cheek and my bottom teeth are up on my forehead.

"Whoa, Ra, you okay?" she whispers.

"Oh no, can you tell?" I pant back. I try rolling my head in a circle. "I don't know why I'm so nervous!"

Mom gets in line at the front desk to sign me in, and Arun climbs into one of the several dozen folding chairs that have been set up in the lobby. He somehow already has a lollipop in his mouth and two more in his hand. Bhai wheels himself down the aisle, waving at one of the tellers behind the counter as though they've been best friends since the beginning of time.

"Ra, you got this. Remember, just be yourself."

"This *is* myself, and myself is a *mess*!" I hiss. I look around the room. Boys, boys, boys everywhere. Boys with perfect smiles. Boys with hair gelled up into flawless little spikes. Boys waving headshots in each other's faces.

None of them looks anywhere near as nervous as I feel.

And none of them is wearing makeup!

"Oh no." Water is pooling into my eyes. I start to wipe my face with my hands, trying to get all the powder off.

"Easy, Ra," Chelsea says.

I follow her over to Bhai, who's rearranging people so we can all sit together. "Excuse me, excuse me, family needing to sit together, please. Please move over a few chairs. Thank you. Thank you very much."

Bags get shuffled and butts shift in seats. A few people grumble in protest. I keep my eyes averted, wishing Bhai would stop calling attention to us.

And then I hear a familiar dad voice say, "See, Justin. There's nothing to be embarrassed about. Rahul's here too."

My eyes travel across the floor and run right into Mr. Emery's penny loafers, the edges of his white athletic ankle socks peeking over his shoes. Next to him stands Justin, clasping a picture of himself against his chest that's so perfect I bet he didn't have to edit it at all.

"Oh. Hey, Rahul." Justin's bangs half hide his eyes.

"*You're* here?" My voice comes out all wobbly.

"Why aren't you at football rehearsals?"

"You mean practice?" Justin raspberries his lips and his bangs flutter up a bit. "My mom's making me do this."

Mr. Emery claps the back of Justin's neck, and Justin stands up tall. "You may not be able to tell now," Mr. Emery says, smiling, "but Mrs. Emery was *quite* the superstar herself back in the day. She was a model. A *swimsuit* model. You know, for those department-store mailers in the Sunday newspaper?" He winks at Bhai. "Let's just say I was the envy of a LOT of the neighborhood men."

Bhai chuckles, but I see him looking around for Mom to save him.

"Anyhoo"—Mr. Emery stuffs his hands into his pockets, and the pleats of his khakis accordion out like balloons—"she's trying to get Justin to follow in her footsteps. Big shoes to fill, right, son?"

Justin shoots me a lopsided grin and rolls his eyes. Behind him, I see Mom politely working her way toward us through a crowd of parents, a piece of paper and one of those free bank pens in her hand.

And then a questioning look flits across Justin's blue eyes.

Why is he staring at me like that?

He squints. "What's that white crusty stuff on your face?"

"Nothing!" I brush at my cheeks.

"It's just a little makeup," Chelsea says.

"It's what?" Justin and his dad ask in unison, and for the first time I see how similar they are. Does this mean Justin will grow up to wear pleated pants and penny loafers with ankle socks?

Please, God. No.

"Dan, hi," Mom interrupts us. "How are you? How's Lisa?"

"Oh, she's good. We're good," Mr. Emery says. "She wanted to come, but Justin begged and begged to have *me* bring him instead." He covers half his mouth with his hand. "I guess she was being too much of a stage mom!" He goes to tousle Justin's hair, but he ducks out of the way. "She'll be sorry she missed you. And Rahul, we never see you anymore!" He smiles at me. "You should come over!"

Justin shifts back and forth on his feet uncomfortably.

Justin and I have lived in the same neighborhood since we were in kindergarten. When we were younger, he'd sometimes come over to my place, or

I'd go over there. One summer, the Emerys got an inflatable pool for their backyard, and they used to joke that the two of us were like minnows, because we'd stay in the water all day long.

But then, I don't know. Things changed.

"Yeah, we'll have to get the kids together," Mom says. She puts an arm around my shoulder. "Hey, Rahul, we need to fill out this information form before the audition."

"Wait, there's a form?" Mr. Emery spins Justin toward the front desk. "I must have my head screwed on backward! Come on, son, let's get you all signed in."

Justin shoots me an awkward thumbs-up over his shoulder and says, "Break a leg." Then he grins. "But, you know, not like you did at football."

I know he's joking, but I cringe anyway. Then Mom, Chelsea, and I slide into the chairs that Bhai and Arun have been guarding with their lives.

CHAPTER 17

Mom takes a first stab at the information sheet and then hands it to Chelsea and me to fill in the "hobbies" section.

"I really think you should work the numbers angle." Chelsea chews on her pinky nail. "So, put down math."

"Hold on." I peruse the answers Mom's written in and shake my head. Mom may be one of the smartest people I know, but this won't do.

She went and answered every question truthfully. And in pen.

I scratch out all her answers and put the *correct* ones next to them.

Height: ~~4'6"~~ 4'9"

Weight: ~~78 LBS~~. 88 LBS.

Hair color: ~~Black~~ DARK BROWN

Eye color: ~~Brown~~ HAZEL

Build: ~~Slim~~ ATHLETIC

"Okay. I'm ready." I suck on the end of the pen and look up at Chelsea.

"Ra," she whispers. Her eyes widen. "Dark brown? Hazel?"

"What? They are! When it's really sunny out!"

She looks doubtful. "Athletic?"

"Who nailed twenty push-ups not so long ago?!"

"Fair. But you know they're going to see you, right?"

"It's not about what *they* see." I chew on the pen again. "It's about what the camera sees."

She sighs. "So what are you going to put for hobbies then? Skydiving? Downhill ski slaloming?"

I pull the pen out of my mouth. "A, how do you know that word, and B, how do you spell it?"

"Ra! Stop it!" She laughs, and for the first time all day I start to relax.

She takes the paper out of my hands and looks it up and down. "I guess these'll do. But honestly, you should just be yourself."

"I am being myself. But, like, better." I smile.

I pull out my headshot and cover it with the information sheet. Hopefully they won't even look at it.

The door to the bank conference room flies open, and a large woman in an emerald-green turtleneck with a shawl wrapped around her shoulders walks out. Her dark red hair is piled on top of her head and held in place by what looks like giant plastic chopsticks.

"Hi, kids!" she says in a deep, throaty voice. "My name is Jean, and I'm your casting director."

I almost stop breathing. A real-life casting director. *In Indiana.*

"I drove in this morning from Indianapolis. It's my first time in, uh"—she grimaces ever so slightly—"Greenville. But I'm so excited to meet all of you."

She doesn't sound that excited.

"So the way this works is"—she clears her throat—"I'll call you in one at a time. You'll hand me your information sheet and headshot on the way in. We'll talk to you and get to know you. And we'll record the whole thing just so we know what you look like on camera. And remember, we really want to see some personality."

I swallow. Personality? I spot Justin and Mr. Emery two rows away from us. Justin's filling in his information sheet while Mr. Emery chats animatedly with the dad sitting to his right. The dad seems to be shrinking away from him.

It's not fair. Justin's light-brown hair hangs perfectly over his face. He scratches the side of his arm just below his short-sleeve T-shirt. Then he scrawls in something on the sheet that makes him quietly chuckle.

Even when he's doing nothing, personality spills out of his every pore.

I glance down at my own dress shirt, the long sleeve buttoned all the way to my wrist, the crisp ironed edge practically screaming, "Look how boring I am!"

"All right." Jean flips up a piece of paper on her clipboard. "Now, who's my first victim?"

Victim?

Jean chuckles, and the room vibrates like a train just passed by. "I'm only kidding. This will be painless. I promise." She smiles, and if I didn't know better, I'd swear I saw two fangs pointing out from under her top lip.

✦ ✦ ✦

With every kid who goes in, my anxiety grows. What are they doing in there? What will *I* do in there?

I've already had to pee three times in the last twenty minutes. With every restroom visit, I emerge with a new hairstyle. I try brushing it down, but by the time I return to the bathroom it's slowly climbing its way back up into the wavy helmet it always is. I try changing the side I part it on, but the look in Chelsea's eyes tells me that it's a no go.

I'm making my way back to my seat for the third time, navigating through the rows of folding chairs, when Jean calls my name.

"Ray-HULL! Do we have a Rayhull Kay-POOR?"

I hear Mom's polite reply. "Rahul Kapoor. He's right here. We're coming."

"Ra! This is it!" Chelsea grabs my arm excitedly.

Mom, Chelsea, and I sidle up to Jean, who's crossing names off the sheet of paper on her clipboard. "Sorry, no groups of three. Only one parent per child. No friends."

"Yeah, but . . ." I can hear the wheels turning in Chelsea's brain. "I'm his coach. His acting coach."

Jean's eyes flit over the top edge of her clipboard and peer down at Chelsea. "Uh-huh. I see. Well, I'm sorry. The room is small and we can only have one person per child. So who's it going to be? Acting coach or mom?"

I look up at Mom. "Can Chelsea come with me?"

Mom hesitates ever so slightly, and then she bends down and squeezes my arm. "Of course. Break a leg!"

"Hup, hup! Gotta stay on schedule." Jean whirls around, her shawl nearly hitting Mom in the face. Chelsea and I follow close on her heels.

The door slams shut behind us and Jean announces, "This is Ray-HULL Kay-POOR. And"—she raises a single eyebrow—"his acting coach."

Chelsea and I giggle nervously as she pushes me toward the empty chair in the middle of the room. I stumble into it and shield my eyes from the enormous lighting instrument glaring at my face.

When my eyes finally adjust, I can make out a long folding table behind the lamp. Three men in suits are seated at it. One is almost entirely bald, except for a ring of gray hair and a few stray strands combed over the top. His skin is so pale it almost glows. One has a neatly trimmed brown mustache and a name tag that says "Hi! I'm Mark!," and the last one on the end is a young-looking man with an easy smile. Next to them, a kid wearing a Greenville Community College hoodie fiddles with a video camera.

"Oh, well this is a nice surprise," the young-looking one on the end of the table says, smiling at me. "How are you?" His voice is deep and friendly. "I'm Wyatt. And it's nice to see someone different for a change. What's your ethnicity, young man?"

Jean darts over to him and whispers in his ear, but the room is so small we can all hear her. "I don't think it's a good idea to ask that. There might be rules. I'm not sure."

He turns to her and chuckles. "Well, I'm African American. Am I allowed to say that?"

The whole room titters nervously.

"I'm American, too," I say, about to launch into my standard response. "But my parents are from—"

"Hup! Hup! None of that!" Jean cuts me off. "Guys, let's try to stay out of trouble here, okay?"

I see the two other men behind the table passing my info sheet back and forth between them. I don't know how Jean would feel about me making any guesses, but I'm pretty sure they're Caucasian. I mean, they're definitely white. Come to think of it, almost everyone in the waiting room was white, too.

The one with the name tag that says "Hi! I'm Mark!" rubs his forehead between his thumb and his finger. "Listen, Rayhull . . ."

"It's Rahul," Chelsea interrupts.

Mark looks at Chelsea. "That's what I said."

"No it's not."

"Don't worry about it." I giggle nervously. "It's fine."

"His name's Rahul. Not Rayhull," Chelsea repeats.

"Right. That's what I'm saying. Rayhull."

"That's not how you—"

"It's okay, Chels!" I interrupt them. The whole room turns my way. "Sorry about that, Mr., um, Mark. Honestly, it's kind of a weird name anyway."

Chelsea looks at me. "No weirder than Mark."

"Listen." Mark keeps his eyes trained on the table, his fingers scratching at an invisible spot. "I want to do the right thing here. I don't want to waste your time. And I don't want to get your hopes up. We probably should have specified this, but"—he glares at Jean—"somehow it didn't make it into the casting announcement.

"In any case," he sighs, "unfortunately, you're not the right . . . How should I say this? You're not the right "type" for this commercial." He makes air quotes around the word *type*.

Jean sticks a finger in each ear. "La, la, la, la, la, la, la. Not listening. Not listening!"

She should meet Arun.

Mark tugs on his tie and keeps going. "We're casting a family, and the parents are going to be . . . Well, they need to look something like this." He holds up a picture of a mom, dad, and boy, all with blond hair and tan skin, in khaki pants and flowy white shirts. They're outside on a bright-green lawn playing with a fluffy golden retriever. "This is the feel of this commercial. I'm sorry."

Jean presses her fingers into her temples.

Wyatt leans across the table. "Mark, I dunno. Maybe we could rethink the spot. If you ask me, this could be a great opportunity for us to get with the picture and start being more inclusive. More diverse."

"I don't disagree with you, Wyatt." Mark starts scratching at that invisible spot on the table again. "But that's not what we're doing here *today*."

"Why not today?" Chelsea asks.

Wyatt stands up at the table. "Smart young lady. It's a good question. Why not today, Mark?"

Jean turns herself into the corner of the room and

presses her face up against the wall, as if she wants to disappear. And then the guy with the gray hair and bald spot stands up and places both his hands on the table.

From the way the room grows quiet, I'm guessing he's in charge.

"Young man." He smiles, maybe just a little too big. "We very much appreciate your coming in. That was a terrific audition. Thank you for your time. We'll be in touch if we decide to cast you."

"A terrific audition?" Chelsea asks incredulously. "He hasn't even done anything!"

They can't kick me out. Not yet.

My mind races desperately for a way to make this work.

"Wait! What if—?" I raise my hand, but my hand is trembling, so I shove it underneath me and sit on it.

I dig into the recesses of my brain. I try to remember everything I read on the internet about acting. Everything Mrs. Daugherty taught us during the musical.

"Every character . . . ," I start to say, hoping that the words will come. I lock eyes with Chelsea, but she has no idea where I'm headed.

And neither do I.

"Every character . . . has to have . . ." This might work. "A backstory." I get out of the chair. "So, my character's backstory. Maybe . . . Um, maybe when I was a little baby, I was abandoned. Like at an orphanage. And . . ."

Now Jean is slowly banging her head against the wall.

I know I'm failing. I'm failing hard. But I say it anyway. "I mean, could I be their adopted son?"

No one will make eye contact with me. Gray Hair is staring at his feet, and Mark is slowly peeling his name tag off his lapel.

Chelsea walks over to me and takes my hand. "Come on, Ra. They don't deserve you."

As we walk past the table, Wyatt mouths, "I'm sorry," and then hangs his head.

CHAPTER 18

As soon as we get back to the van, Mom, Bhai, and Arun barrage us with a million questions.

"It went well," I say. Chelsea just keeps staring out the window, shaking her head. Chelsea and I didn't even have a minute to talk about everything that happened, but somehow, when we got out of that conference room, we both just shut down.

"How do you know?" Arun sticks his head between the headrests.

I want to curl into a little ball, but I do my best to pretend like everything is fine. "Um, I know because the guy who was clearly in charge of the whole thing said, and I quote, 'That was a terrific audition.' So I guess it went pretty well. He said they'd be in touch."

Arun looks suspicious. "Don't they just say that to everyone?"

"No, Arun, they don't! Please don't act like you know *anything* about auditioning, when you clearly don't. They only say it if they like you."

"Everything okay, Chelsea?" Bhai asks, looking over his shoulder.

"Mm-hmm." She nods.

All I want to do is get home and make this whole day go away. I can't believe I ever let myself get excited about this in the first place.

"Did anyone comment on your shirt?" Bhai asks, a smile behind his voice.

"The shirt wasn't the problem," Chelsea mumbles under her breath.

"What was that, Chelsea? Was there a problem?" Mom asks.

"No," I say. "No problem."

Chelsea shoves her knees into the seat back in front of her.

"Hey! No kicking!" Arun whines.

"Are you sure everything's okay?" Mom asks as she pulls the van into Chelsea's neighborhood.

I shake my head no at Chelsea. I don't want to

talk about it. She silently climbs out of the van. And then just before pulling the handle that makes the door slide shut, she plants both her feet firmly on the driveway and says, "They discriminated against Rahul."

"They did *what*?" Mom asks, her eyes searching Chelsea's face.

"No, they didn't, Mom." I look pleadingly at Chelsea. "That's not what happened. Come on." I know she's trying to help, but the last thing I want to do is talk about this. I know I shouldn't, but somehow I feel . . . I don't know. Embarrassed. Or ashamed. Like I should have known better.

Like there's something wrong with me for thinking I could have ever gotten this commercial in the first place.

Now Mr. Wilson is walking down the driveway. The knees of his jeans are covered in dirt, like he's been working in the yard. "Rahul, how'd it go today? Are we gonna get to see you on TV?"

"We'll see!" I try to smile, even though I can feel tears trying to push their way out. "They said they'll call!"

"They're not going to call, Ra." Chelsea looks up at her dad. "They said Rahul wasn't the right type because he wasn't white. They didn't even let him audition."

In the rearview mirror, I see Mom looking back at me. Her brows are knit together, and her eyes are full of worry. I see her tighten her grip on the steering wheel.

Mr. Wilson sets his jaw. "Well, that's not okay. That's not okay at all."

"No, it's not." Mom turns the car off. "Rahul, what happened?"

But I'm too upset now to say anything, so Chelsea tells everyone the whole story. She tells them how Mark couldn't pronounce my name, and Jean acted weird, and the only nice one was Wyatt, but he couldn't do anything.

No one says a word the whole way home from Chelsea's house to ours, but after I help Bhai up the driveway, Mom quietly takes me by the hand and walks me back out to the van.

"What are we doing?" I ask, buckling up my seat belt.

"We're going back," Mom says, and I can feel the anger coursing through her body. "We're going to have a talk with those bank people."

"No, Mom, I don't want to—"

"Rahul. You had every right to be there. They should have let you audition. It's okay to stand up for yourself," she says as we back out of the driveway. Then, she repeats, "It's okay to stand up for yourself, and it's important to stand up for what's right."

By the time we return to the bank, the parking lot is a wasteland. The sky is black, and the streetlights cast long shadows of trees over the empty parking spaces. Mom doesn't even park in an actual spot. She just pulls right up to the front door. She leaves the car running and tells me to wait while she sees if anyone's there. Then she gets out and walks up the stairs.

From the passenger seat, I watch her look through the sliding glass doors. The entire bank is dark, bathed only in dim emergency lights. I squint, and I can just make out the blurry outline of someone vacuuming the carpet.

And then I see the strangest thing. Mom, who's always so put together, who manages to get me, Dad, and Arun out the door every morning, who's the only person who can make the entire Auntie Squad stop their squabbling with a gentle word, loses her temper.

She pounds her fists over and over and over against the "Caution Automatic Door" sign. Her back shakes as she screams, "OPEN UP I WANT TO TALK TO

SOMEBODY!" at the top of her lungs. But the person cleaning the carpets doesn't even look up.

I know Mom's right. And I know she wants to do this. But I hate that she has to.

Because of me.

I just want to go home.

That night, after dinner, Arun and I sit on the steps and do our best to eavesdrop on Mom and Dad doing the dishes.

"What can you do, Sarita? That's just how things are. We can't change the whole system."

"Well, we can try. First thing tomorrow morning, I'm going back and demanding an explanation."

"They already *gave* an explanation. It's just an explanation we don't like."

"Which is why we have to keep pushing, Anish."

A handful of silverware clatters against the side of the sink. Arun and I lean in.

Dad's voice gets really soft. "All right, it's a plan. I'll come with you."

Then it sounds like Dad's footsteps are headed in our direction, so Arun and I clamber up the stairs like squirrels.

✦ ✦ ✦

Mom and Dad went back to the bank the next morning without me. They told me they wanted to have a conversation "between adults" first. When they got home, they said that we should hear more soon. A few days later, we got a letter in the mail:

Dear Dr. and Mrs. Kapoor:

We appreciate your bringing to our attention your concerns regarding your son's recent audition for our advertising campaign to promote our No-Fee Checking Accounts. Your allegations were given our utmost consideration.*

We would like to assure you that we have made a full investigation into the matter, and that we have found no wrongdoing by any of our employees or anyone who was contracted to work for us at the time of the alleged incident. No racial prejudices or biases played any role in our casting process, and Greenville People's Bank is 100 percent committed to equal-opportunity employment practices.

In the end a decision was made to cast a professional actor with several commercial credits. While we appreciated Rahul's audition, we ended up casting the most experienced actor for the role.

Sincerely,
Robert Plouffe
President
Greenville People's Bank

***Our No-Fee Checking Account promotion is good for the next six months, should you wish to take advantage of it.**

"Well then," Mom said, tossing the letter into the trash. "Looks like we'll be taking our money to a new bank."

CHAPTER 19

I figure Justin will want to know who got the part, so the next day at morning assembly, I muster up the courage to leave the front row and make my way to the back of the room, where all the cool kids congregate.

The cool-kids' area is like a nightmare except your eyes are still open. I almost get knocked over by two guys wrestling, and I have to dodge a cheese puff that goes whizzing by my head. It wasn't even aimed at me.

Trina Drexel is passing around a glitter-filled lip-gloss pen to a bunch of girls, and in the center of it all, Brent is holding court to a captive audience of kids, including Justin. "Check it out." He thrusts his phone into their faces. "Greatest Hail Mary of all time!"

I try to get Justin's attention, but he's mesmerized by Brent's phone. I poke my head in.

"Ooh, I love a good Hail Mary!" I say, grateful that I still remember some stuff from *Football for Dummies*. My voice catches in my throat, but I plow ahead. "Is this a video of *the* game?" People who watch football never actually say *which* game they're watching; they just call it "the game."

"Why are you *here*?" Brent pockets his phone, and the rest of the guys suddenly get very interested in their fingernails. He grabs the lip gloss out of Trina's hand and makes his voice all falsetto-y. "Did you need some of this? Chelsea didn't bring some for you today?"

"What? No!" I clutch the straps of my backpack. I try to whisper, but everyone's watching us. "Listen, that stuff in the bathroom wasn't what you thought."

Brent raises an eyebrow and plays dumb. "You mean the part where you were putting on makeup or the part where you told me you make out with your mom?"

Trina swipes her lip gloss back, and Brent is

momentarily distracted. I quickly try to change subjects. "Anyway, I just came here to tell Justin something."

"So who's stopping you?" Brent slides a chair out for me. I go to sit, but my book bag gets caught on the back of the chair. I have to catch myself from falling.

"Easy, dude," Brent says. "Don't sprain your ankle again." Then he coughs into his fist. "For Justin."

A couple of the guys laugh.

"What?" I cringe and my face feels hot. Coming here was a big mistake. I wish I could just leave now.

Justin looks up at Brent and shakes his head. Then he turns to me. "Hey, do you wanna just talk later?"

"Why?" Brent slaps the kid sitting next to him on the shoulder. "Do you guys need *alone* time?" Now some of the girls start to giggle, too.

I rub my sweaty palms on the front of my pants. I steel myself and look right at Justin. I try not to notice how blue his eyes look. "I just came here to say, I'm sorry you didn't get the commercial. But, honestly, I don't think there was any way you could have gotten it anyhow."

An uneasy look flickers across Justin's face. Brent silently mouths a huge "WHA?"

"My mom found out from the bank that they cast some professional actor who's done like a ton of commercials. He probably didn't even live in Greenville. I just thought you'd want to know."

Justin looks like he wants to crawl under a rock.

"WHOA! WHOA! WHOA!" Brent jumps between us. "What is he talking about? What commercial?"

"It's nothing." Justin drops his head back and covers his eyes with his hand. "It was just this dumb audition my mom made me go to."

"You went to some audition thing with *Rahul*?"

"I didn't go with Rahul."

"But you auditioned for something together?"

Justin sits back up and leans forward in his chair. "Would you just stop it, Brent?"

"Good morning, everyone!" Principal Jacobson's voice cuts through the air over the PA system just as the morning bell rings. "Let's all settle down. I want to get through announcements quickly, because we have some very special guests with us today!"

Brent glares at me and then slides down into his chair.

Shoot. Assembly has officially started. Now I'm stuck here. I look for the back of Chelsea's head in the front row, but there are too many people between us.

"Oh wow!" I hear Trina whisper next to me. "Those dresses are awesome!"

I look up to the stage, and my hand reflexively clutches my shirt into a tight fist right over my heart.

If I thought the cool-kids' section was a nightmare, then this is a zombie apocalypse.

"I wonder if I could get one of those at the mall?" Trina asks.

Filing up onto the stage, next to Principal Jacobson at the podium, are Urvi Auntie, Mona Auntie, and Nandita Auntie. And they're wearing saris. Saris in every color of the rainbow.

And bringing up the rear is Juhi Auntie, carrying a giant poster board that says "International Bazaar."

CHAPTER 20

I scan the room, looking for other aunties who might come popping up onto the stage like sari-clad ninjas. But I don't see any.

If the aunties are here, does that mean Mom is, too?

Of course not, I tell myself. She dropped us off at school *on her way to work.*

But why wouldn't she have told me that the Auntie Squad was going to be at morning assembly today? And why are they here anyway?

Please, please, please don't embarrass me, I pray. I will myself not to look at Brent.

Principal Jacobson starts in with the morning

announcements. Where to meet the bus for the away debate match, blah blah blah, some decision the PTA voted on about sports teams and fund-raising, blah blah blah, and how we all need to be better about picking up trash after lunch. Blah.

Trina and her entourage are still talking about the saris. "Are those *peacocks* on her dress? That's so cute!"

I glance at the clock. Morning assembly isn't that long. There's not that much time left before the first-period bell will ring. Principal Jacobson flips up the paper on her clipboard, and I breathe a sigh of relief as I realize she's still not done with her endless drone.

Maybe, just maybe, this will all be okay.

Or maybe not. Nandita Auntie gets up from her chair and taps Principal Jacobson on the shoulder. Her sari is covered in so many sequins that she looks like a human-sized disco ball.

With Coke-bottle glasses on top.

"Is it almost our turn? I want to make sure we have enough time." She's trying to keep her voice down, but it's Nandita Auntie. Even if there wasn't a microphone up there, we'd all be able to hear her.

A bunch of kids start to giggle, and Principal Jacobson tells us all to simmer down. She flips up another page on her clipboard. "I just need a few more minutes. There are so many things to cover . . ." She trails off as her eyes dart back and forth across the paper.

Come on! I silent-scream inside my head. *Read more announcements!*

"You know what?" She looks up. "These can wait until tomorrow."

She sticks the clipboard under her arm and leans into the microphone. "Students, let's give a warm welcome to Mrs. Juhi Shah. She and her friends have come here today to talk to you about a very special event, the International Bazaar."

Principal Jacobson takes a few steps back, but Juhi Auntie stays glued to her spot, a look of terror plastered across her face. Nandita Auntie scurries behind her, her sari shimmering like a mirage, and pushes her toward the podium. "Come on, Juhi, you can do it!" we all hear her say, and another round of giggles boils over.

Juhi Auntie trips up to the microphone, and her movement makes the bright-green peacocks on her deep-blue sari do a little dance.

Brent kicks the back of Justin's chair and snickers. "Are those birds making out?"

I bury my face in my hands, willing this to end.

Juhi Auntie hands Nandita Auntie the poster board, which she holds up over her head. It says "International Bazaar," and underneath the title are five numbered bullet points.

1. **This April!**
2. **A Festival Celebrating Our Diverse Cultures**
3. **Performances and Food from Around the World**
4. **Please Take a Flyer**
5. **Volunteer Opportunities**

Juhi Auntie mumbles something into the microphone, but it just sounds like a bunch of *s*'s and *f*'s coming through the speakers. Three hundred Greenville Junior High students lean forward.

Nandita Auntie reaches over and bends the microphone closer to Juhi Auntie's still terrified face. But now Juhi Auntie is completely frozen.

"It's fine, Juhi! I'll do it!" Nandita Auntie bellows. She steps in front of the podium.

"I think you can all hear me without the microphone, right? Hi, kids! We are *so* excited to be here!

My name is Mrs. Nandita Patel. Behind the podium is Mrs. Juhi Shah, and my other friends are Mrs. Mona Rao and Mrs. Urvi Agrawal."

Mona Auntie and Urvi Auntie wave hello to us.

"We're here to tell you about the International Bazaar!" Nandita Auntie's face lights up. "We only have a few minutes, so we'll just stick to our talking points! Juhi—hold the poster."

Juhi Auntie raises the poster over her head, clutching it tight to keep it from trembling in her hands. Nandita Auntie points to bullet point number one.

"It's this April! So, yes, we do have some time, but as I'm sure Principal Jacobson teaches you"—she nods at her—"never, ever procrastinate! Why do tomorrow what you can do today? Am I right?"

She tosses out "Am I right?" as if she expects a response. There isn't one.

"Okay, well, no worries. Since it's not until April, maybe we'll come back again, and you can show me your audience participation skills the next time!"

She laughs at herself, prompting Urvi Auntie and Mona Auntie to laugh as well, like they're her backup act or something.

"Number two!" she goes on. "It is a festival celebrating our diversity! A chance to learn about all the different cultures from around the world that have come together here in our little town of Greenville. My friends and I are all of Indian heritage, but the festival will showcase *all* of the countries from around the world!"

I look out at the sea of mostly white students in the assembly hall. I wouldn't call Nandita Auntie a liar or anything, but there's no way every country from around the world will be represented there. There were only, like, five last year.

"*How* will we celebrate our diversity?" she asks, beckoning the audience to respond with her outstretched hand.

Two kids shyly shout back, "How?" making Nandita Auntie go nuts. She claps her hands so wildly the sequins on her sari cast glittery squares all over the ceiling.

"Great question! By doing number three! We will have a cultural show with dance and music and art! And there will be a food buffet with dishes from every country under the sun! Now, I want you to go home and tell your parents all about it, and see if they want to cook something for the Bazaar."

Principal Jacobson looks down at her watch and signals Nandita Auntie to wrap it up.

"Oh, right." Nandita Auntie shoots her an annoyed look before turning back to us. "How will your parents know about it, you ask?"

This time a dozen or so people holler back, "How?"

Nandita Auntie couldn't look more pleased. "You are such quick learners! Well, we will be handing out flyers for you to take home to share with your families! Becaaaaauuussseeee . . ." She stretches the word out for an impossibly long time. I try to make myself as small as possible, hoping that no one will associate me with her.

"Because we want you all to think about number five! Volunteering! We'll need help with setup and food service and cleanup, and running the stage, and of course, if any of you have a talent you want to share from your home country, we want you to sign up for the cultural program. So don't forget to take a flyer!"

And finally, the bell rings. I clutch my backpack and hop out of the chair, but Principal Jacobson sprints to the microphone, nearly knocking Juhi Auntie out of the way. "Everyone stay seated! You are not dismissed." She waits for the room to settle, then looks at Nandita Auntie. "Now, Mrs. Patel, I think you forgot the most important part."

Nandita Auntie stares at the poster board in Juhi Auntie's hands. "No, I didn't. I did all five bullet points." Then, as if she'd just walked into her own surprise birthday party, she cups both her hands over her cheeks and howls, "You're right, I did! The reason we're here today in the first place is that this year's International Bazaar will be held RIGHT HERE! At the Greenville Junior High football field!"

I almost fall out of the chair.

Is it too late to transfer to another school?

CHAPTER 21

Now I understand why the cool kids sit in the back.

As soon as we're officially dismissed, I'm the first person out of the room. Mr. Hayden holds the door open, a stack of flyers in his hand.

"Here you go, Rahul." He hands me one.

"No thanks. I already know all about it." I step to the side to wait for Chelsea.

When she finally comes out, she takes not one, but about a dozen flyers from Mr. Hayden.

Out of the corner of my eye, I see the Auntie Squad heading for the open door. I try to usher Chelsea along.

"Oh, hi, Chelsea!" My heart drops as I hear Nandita Auntie's voice. Ugh. Caught. "Hi, Rahul beta," she chirps. "How cute you two are together!" The Squad corners us in front of a row of lockers.

"Chelsea!" Mona Auntie pops her head in from behind Nandita Auntie. "Rahul's mom and I spoke! I'm so excited you want to perform at the Bazaar. I have your dad's number, so I'll be in touch, okay?"

Mr. Hayden interrupts us. "I'm so sorry, ladies, but these two need to start heading to class."

The aunties start to disperse, but not before Nandita Auntie grabs a handful of my cheek between her fingers.

As we head down the hall to our lockers, I turn to Chelsea. "Are you going to hand out *all* of those?"

She shrugs. "I don't know. Maybe. I'm getting kind of excited about it now." She hands me one. "Want one?"

I force myself to take the flyer from her. "Sure. Thanks." I slide it into my book bag and zip it shut.

CHAPTER 22

I'm in my room doing my homework when I hear Mom come home.

I run down the stairs and intercept her in the foyer. I hand her the flyer.

"Mom, did you know the aunties were coming to assembly today? Did you know the Bizarre is going to be at my school?"

She takes the flyer and casually heads toward the kitchen. "Oh good." She peruses it. "Juhi found a venue!"

"Yeah, the venue is *my* school!"

She sets the flyer on the kitchen table. "Oh, I'm so glad! What a perfect place to have the Bazaar."

Arun has made his way into the kitchen now. "The Bazaar is going to be at your school?" He points at me. "Hahahahaha!"

"Mom? Did you see that? I'm never gonna live this down! Did you know they were coming to assembly today? Mona Auntie, Nandita Auntie, Juhi Auntie, *and* Urvi Auntie! They all wore saris and tried to get the whole middle school to volunteer!"

"Rahul." Mom pinches Arun's cheek and pours herself a glass of water. "First, I didn't know they were coming to your school today, but I don't need to know everything. The venue is Juhi's responsibility, and it sounds like she got her entire committee to come."

She takes a sip of her water.

"Second"—she narrows her eyes at me—"does it *bother* you they wore saris?"

I'm not sure how to answer her. It did bother me. But I don't really know *why* it bothered me. I guess having the Auntie Squad onstage, dressed like that, saying, "Look at us! We're from India!" just made me feel, I don't know, even more different from everybody else than I already feel.

But I don't want to tell Mom that. So instead I say, "It doesn't bother *me*. But Mom, you should have heard what all the other kids were saying."

She takes another sip of water. "Why? What were they saying?"

"They said . . . well, they . . ." I think about Trina and the other girls. But now all I remember is that they thought the saris were awesome and wanted to know if they could buy them at the mall. I consider telling her what Brent said about the peacocks making out, but now it just seems dumb.

"I guess they didn't say anything."

She sits down at the table. "Rahul, the Bazaar is a cultural festival, so they were celebrating our culture. I'm sure that's why they wore their saris. I don't think they meant to embarrass you."

"I'm not embarrassed," I mumble.

"Think about it this way. If your classmates come, they'll get to learn more about India, and you can learn more about where their families come from."

"Mom, most of my classmates come from right here!"

She ignores me. "Plus, Dad's band is playing." She pokes at my rib cage jokingly. "Which means all your friends will get to hear Bollywood Supply. Won't that be nice?"

Arun's face looks like it might skyrocket off his

head. "Yeah, Rahul, won't that be nice? Dad's band is gonna play at your school!"

Oh, God. I hadn't even thought about that.

Right on cue, Dad waltzes through the front door, his keys clattering into the key bowl.

"Anish," Mom calls, "it's all set—Juhi got Rahul's school for the Bazaar! Only a few more months for you guys to practice." She waggles her eyebrows at me. "Rahul is so excited!"

After dinner, I excuse myself to do the last of my homework. All that's left is some geometry. I drag my bag over, pull out my math book, and lean up against the side of the bed.

But I can't focus.

In a few months both Mom *and* Dad are going to be performing. At my school.

What if people come?

What if Brent comes?

I look down at my foot, and I spin my ankle around. It's almost 100 percent now, but looking at it just reminds me of how awful I did at football tryouts.

And I'm not going to be on TV anytime soon.

I still haven't found anything to be the best at.

I look over at my alarm clock and find myself tracing the power cord with my eyes. I follow it to where it disappears behind my bed skirt, and my chest starts to clench. Is my bed skirt too close to the outlet? And if it is, is that a fire hazard?

I reach behind my bed and pull the plug out.

Then I walk to the foot of the bed and tug on the bottom of the bed frame. It's heavy. I tug harder, and it moves away from the wall a few inches. I get up on top of the bed and scooch up to my pillow. I peer down at the space between the wall and the bed.

It seems far enough away now.

I get off the bed and plug the alarm clock back in, and for a moment I feel okay. But then I hesitate. *Is* it far enough away? I force my arm behind the bed and wave my hand between the wall and the bed skirt. That's got to be plenty of space, right?

Or is it?

Stop worrying about it, I tell myself.

I stare at my math book. But now all I can think about is that plug and how close my bed skirt is and what if I accidentally set the whole house on fire?

Should I unplug it again?

I ball my fists. What is happening to me? And why can't I stop it?

All I know is, I have to get out of here.

I tear myself out of the bedroom and run down to the den to watch TV with Bhai.

"Hi, Bhai," I say, stepping around his folded-up wheelchair and climbing onto the couch next to him.

"Oh, hi, Rahul." He looks my way. "Are you okay?"

"Uh-huh." I nod. "What are you watching?"

"This movie called *The Man Who Knew Infinity*."

"No Bollywood tonight?" My voice comes out a little shaky, but talking to Bhai is already calming me down. I steady my breath.

"I've already seen all the Bollywood movies they were showing on the Indian movie channel," he says. "But this film is good. It has that actor from *Slumdog Millionaire* in it. Have you heard of it?"

"No. What is it?" I take in Dev Patel on the TV screen. He's in a temple in India, scratching math formulas on the floor in chalk. He's wearing a dhoti.

"It's about this very famous mathematician from India, Srinivasa Ramanujan, who lived during the time of British rule. He was accepted to Cambridge University in England. But when he got to England, he encountered a lot of prejudice. Racism. But, you know, he didn't give up. And after he died, people realized just how brilliant he was. Today, the whole world recognizes him as one of the greatest mathematicians who ever lived."

"Hmm," I say. The way Bhai talks about math, it doesn't seem so nerdy.

I look over at him. He's staring down at his lap, picking at his wool pants.

"Everything all right?" I ask.

Bhai smiles at me. "I was just remembering your grandmother and thinking how some things never change. Ramanujan had to face bullying in the early 1900s. And your grandmother faced the same types of things some fifty years later."

He beckons me a little closer on the couch and slides his arm around my shoulder. Then he says more quietly, "And I'm thinking about you. And what happened to you at that audition."

I shrug. "They were just being honest. I mean, the kid had to be white."

Bhai pauses, looking at me. "But *why* did he have to be white, Rahul? Or more importantly, why do you *agree* he had to be white?"

"Because the parents were white." I have a feeling that Bhai isn't satisfied with my answer. "I mean, doesn't that make sense?"

"Well, okay, so the parents were white. But like

that man said, maybe they could have thought of a different commercial. Maybe they need to start opening up their way of thinking. Your mom and dad are customers at that bank, right? They're not white. So why does the family in the commercial have to be white?"

"You mean Mom and Dad *used* to be customers at that bank." I lean my head back against Bhai's arm.

"That's right!" Bhai chuckles, threatening to let out one of his full-on belly laughs. "They showed them, didn't they?"

I like the way Bhai's cardigan still has a trace smell of something that makes me picture India. Like a smoky fire on a dirt road. Or spicy pickles. He's probably washed his sweater like a million times, but it always smells like, well, Bhai.

"Anyway, it doesn't really matter." I scrunch up my toes, which are dangling over the edge of the sofa. My socks wrinkle up against my feet. I imagine the picture of the parents they showed me in the audition, and their perfect blond kid. "Kids like Justin always get to do that kinda stuff anyway. Not kids like me."

"Oh, did something change? Is Justin doing the commercial now?"

"Well, no. He didn't get it either. But you know what I mean."

"No. I don't know what you mean. What *do* you mean?"

I writhe away from his arm a little. "It's just. Ugh. I don't know. You know, *kids like Justin.* They just . . . they always get everything!"

Bhai eyes me, and the creases on the sides of his mouth look deeper than I remember. "Is *that* why you wanted to play football? Were you trying to be more like Justin?"

"No." I shake my head, although I'm not sure if I'm being honest. "I just wanted to do something cool for once."

Bhai and I don't say anything for a little bit. On the television, Dev Patel is now racing across a courtyard in England in a tan suit with two books under his arm.

"Do you *like* Justin?" Bhai finally asks.

I shrug. "He's nice to me." I keep watching the TV.

"Right, right. I guess I meant . . . Well, Rahul, do you . . . I meant, do you *like* . . ." Bhai's voice trails off, and something about the way he pauses makes my stomach queasy.

He pats my head. "Enough talking. Let's finish the movie, huh?"

CHAPTER 23

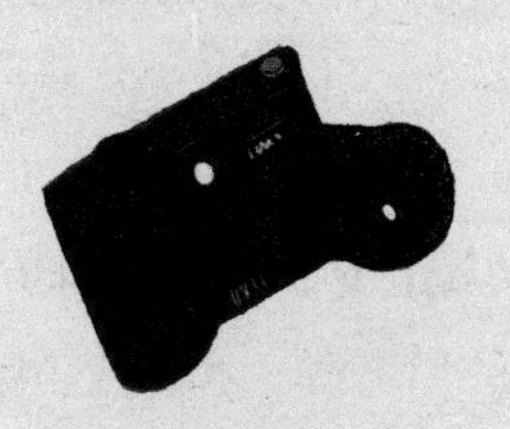

That night, it feels like sleep will never come.

I've moved my bed even farther away from the wall, and I'm staring at my alarm clock, trying to catch that split second when the *11* in 10:11 will turn into the *12* in 10:12. But after what seems like an eternity, I give up. I pull the covers over my eyes and squeeze them shut.

Still no sleep.

I push the covers back down and eye the walkie-talkie on my nightstand, half hoping that I'll hear, "Bhai to Rahul!" and we'll sneak back to the den to watch another movie.

Except that it's a school night, and Mom already

let me stay up late to finish *The Man Who Knew Infinity*. And Bhai's probably snoring away peacefully just like everyone else.

I sigh, and my breath echoes back at me through the silence. I look at the clock, and now somehow twenty minutes has gone by. It's 10:32. Which means if I don't fall asleep *right now*, I'm going to be exhausted tomorrow. Ugh.

I flip over onto my side and hug my pillow. Why was Bhai asking me all those questions about Justin?

I close my eyes and bury my face in the pillow, trying to shut everything out.

Then I picture the way Justin pushed back at Brent in morning assembly. The way he said, "Would you just stop it, Brent?"

I smile.

Wait. What am I doing?

I sit straight up in the bed, the covers falling down to my waist and the pillow tumbling onto the floor.

I have to stop thinking about Justin.

My stomach is all tied up in knots. I'm never going to fall asleep now.

I remember all those weeks ago when I overheard Mom and Dad talking in the kitchen. The way Dad said, "You must see the same things I see."

What does Dad see?

I think about Mom's fists banging the door to the locked-up bank.

That's why I keep thinking about Justin, I tell myself.

Because everything would be easier if I were him. If I weren't ME.

I close my eyes and try to imagine actually turning into Justin. My arms and legs get a little bit longer. And I'm not so skinny.

And I'm white.

I throw the covers back and get all the way out of bed. Ugh. Ugh. Ugh. It's 12:02! *In the morning.* Am I ever going to sleep?

I wave my hand between the wall outlet and the bed skirt.

Then I throw myself facedown into the pillow and clench my eyes shut.

CHAPTER 24

I don't know exactly when I fell asleep, but I wake up to the sound of Arun banging on my bedroom door.

Arun, who is always the last one ready, yelling, "Come on, Rahul! You're going to make us late."

I'm so tired the whole way to school that I can barely keep my eyes open. Chelsea has to remind me to grab my backpack as we climb out of the van, and Mom calls out behind me, "Not even going to say goodbye today?"

I'm still feeling disoriented after assembly as I dig through my locker. So when Justin comes up beside me, I almost jump out of my skin.

“Hey,” he says. He glances furtively around the empty hall, as if he doesn’t want to be seen.

“Hi.” I shove my backpack between my knees and my locker. I try to focus on jamming my notebook into it.

“Um, listen,” he says. “I just . . . I just wanted to say sorry. About all that stuff at assembly yesterday. It was just that Brent . . .”

“Yeah, well, Brent just hates me. He’ll always hate me.”

Justin shakes his head. “He doesn’t . . .” He pauses. “I mean, he’s really not that bad.”

“Yeah, right,” I grumble.

And maybe because I’m tired, or maybe because I know the bell’s going to ring, or who knows why, but I just blurt out, “You know, everyone doesn’t have it as easy as you and Brent do! Not all of us have the whole school cheering for us just ’cause we catch some stupid ball on the football field. You have no idea what it’s like to be me.”

He doesn’t say anything, and now I can’t look at him.

“Sorry,” I finally say, more quietly. “I should have just found you later instead of bothering you in front of everyone anyway. I wasn’t trying to embarrass you.

I just thought you'd want to know about the commercial, but I guess you don't care."

Neither of us says anything. Then Justin slowly exhales through his nose. "You didn't embarrass me. I mean, I was embarrassed, but . . ." He looks at the ground. "It's just because that whole audition thing made me *so* nervous. That's why I didn't want anyone to know about it."

"Really?" I ask.

Justin, nervous? I can't believe he's telling me this.

I turn toward him. "Honestly? I was nervous too. In fact, I made my grandfather iron two shirts for me."

"Oh yeah?" He smiles.

"Yeah. And remember that white stuff on my face? Chelsea put makeup on me because I was sweating so much!"

At first I worry that I've revealed too much. But then he deadpans, "I thought you looked kind of like a ghost." And before I have time to feel embarrassed, we both burst out laughing.

"We better get to class," he says, stuffing his hands into his jeans pockets.

"Yup." I look into my bag to make sure I have

everything. I quickly do a mental checklist: Science book. Check. Math book. Check.

Wait? Math book?

"Oh no." I clench my backpack. "I never did the geometry homework! I started it last night, and then I completely forgot!"

"Well, do it at lunch. Math's not till last period."

I slide down to the floor and throw the book open, right there in the hallway. "No! What is wrong with me? You don't understand. I *never* forget to do my homework. I'm doing it now. Right now."

"Dude, the bell's gonna go off in, like, a second. Just do it later."

I fish my notebook out of my backpack. "Wait, wait. What was the assignment?" Panic is flooding my stomach.

"It was the chapter-five review questions."

I flip to the end of chapter five. There are only three questions. I can do it.

"Come on, Rahul. We're gonna be late!"

I'm scribbling furiously in my notebook.

"I'm gonna go," he says. But he doesn't move. I can feel him staring at me.

Question two, done.

Question three . . .

The bell goes off.

Done.

"Let's go!" Justin yells. "Do you always do your math homework that fast?" he asks as we tear down the hall.

"It wasn't that hard." My breath is ragged as I try to keep up with him.

"Yeah it was. I did it last night. And it was hard. It was *really* hard. Honestly, you're really good at that. That was amazing!"

"You think?" I ask.

A little firework goes off in my heart. I *am* really good at it.

And Justin Emery thinks that's amazing.

The rest of the day I feel like I'm walking on clouds. English, science, and history whiz by. Even in PE, I'm only the *third*-to-last person picked for dodgeball teams.

I feel like I could do anything. The world is my oyster. If I ate oysters, which I don't. My family's vegetarian. But you know what I mean.

And then, it's the last period of the day. Math with Mr. Hayden. When class ends, I linger behind for a second, telling Chelsea I'll meet her in the parking lot.

"You need something, Rahul?" Mr. Hayden asks.

"Um. Well, I had a question . . . ," I start. Now that the moment is here, I feel the slightest hesitation. This was the one thing I was sure I *didn't* want to do. But here I am.

"What's up?" Mr. Hayden taps the stack of homework against his desk, lining up the edges of the papers.

My stomach starts to tie up in little knots. Will this make me even more of a nerd?

"Everything okay, Rahul?"

"Yeah. Um. I was just wondering. Is it too late to join the Mathletes?"

A twinkle forms in Mr. Hayden's eye. "Too late? No. Not at all. Early practices have already started, but we still need people, and things don't really heat up until after the holiday break anyway."

"Is that right?" I ask.

"Uh-huh," he says. "Why, are you interested in joining?"

I smile a little more confidently than I feel.

"Yes." I nod. "I'd like to. If I still can."

"Well, this is great news! You've missed some

stuff, but I think you can jump right in. We've got a great group so far. Jenny Ikeda, Gina Carvallo, and David Nguyen have already joined. Oh, and I'll send you a calendar with the practice schedule to share with your parents. They'll need to sign a permission slip since we have to travel to the district competition. Also, I'll need your T-shirt size. We're getting team T-shirts, and . . ."

My eyes must start to glaze over a little, because Mr. Hayden slows down and breaks into a chuckle.

"It's great to have you, Rahul." He reaches across his desk to shake my hand. "We need to recruit a few more kids, which I'm confident we can do at the Activities Fair. But even with the team right now, I really think this could be the first year in the history of Greenville that we make it to states."

And just like that, that weird feeling in the pit of my stomach disappears.

CHAPTER 25

"Come join the Mathletes!" Gina Carvallo is screaming at the top of her lungs.

She, David, Jenny, and I are camped out behind a folding table in Baker's Hall. All the chairs have been cleared out of the way for the Activities Fair.

The fair is supposed to get everyone excited about second-semester offerings before school closes for the holidays. But truth be told, our school doesn't offer that many activities in the first place, and most kids just sign up for the same old stuff they always do.

But everyone gets to skip last period to attend, so it feels like a party.

"Help us annihilate Prairieville!" Gina screams

again, trying to be heard over kids from all the other clubs screaming just as loud. I thought I'd be more embarrassed to be at the Mathletes table, but I have to admit, it feels pretty good to be part of a group.

"Why all the Prairieville hate?" I ask.

Jenny slumps her shoulders. "Because they've won districts the last three years in a row. They're, like, impossible to beat."

"Totally impossible." Gina looks at me. "Like, next-level impossible."

"Huh," I say, nodding. "What makes them so good?"

"Hot cider, anyone? I got an extra." Mr. Hayden walks over carrying two paper cups in his hands. "Mrs. Daugherty made some cookies, too. They're at the spring musical table, if you want to go grab some." He pulls a cookie wrapped in waxed paper out of his jacket pocket. It's decorated like a snowman. "I think she's a little overeager for winter break. Not that I blame her."

"Ooh, cookies!" David and Gina reach for it at the same time. Their hands collide. David grins. "Fine, it's all yours!"

"Why don't I go grab us a few more?" I offer. I want to go find Chelsea anyway.

I weave in and out of all the other students, being extra careful to duck when I pass the wrestling team area, where Brent's standing on the table doing body-building poses. Ugh. I make my way over to Chelsea.

Chelsea had suggested to Mona Auntie that they have an International Bazaar table at the fair, and lo and behold, here they are.

"Ra! Yay!" She waves as I walk up. "Finally, a customer! No one has stopped by yet!" Mona Auntie's next to her, setting out clipboards for student volunteers to sign up on. She's wearing a pantsuit, and I know I shouldn't, but I feel slightly relieved that—without a whole gaggle of aunties in saris—she blends right in.

Also, I'm secretly happy that no one is coming by to sign up.

"Wanna walk with me?" I ask Chelsea. "I'm on a mission to get cookies."

"Wait, there are cookies? Fun. Would that be okay, Mona Auntie? Can I walk around a bit?"

"Sure, sure. Go find some people to volunteer for us! Tell your friends we want them to be in the show!" Mona Auntie waves us off.

Chelsea and I cut around the perimeter of the room, toward the spring musical table. "How's

Mathletes?" she asks. "Any new people sign up yet?"

"No. Not yet."

"Hmm." She toys with the sleeve of her sweater. "Who else is at your booth?"

"Just the team. And Mr. Hayden. Why?"

"No reason." She sucks her lower lip. "I mean, should I maybe stop by and say hi?"

"Why would you want to do that?"

"No reason."

"Rahul! Chelsea!" Trina's waving at us from behind the Sadie Hawkins table. "Do you guys want to put an idea into our idea jar? To help us pick this year's Sadie Hawkins theme?"

We stop at her table.

Last year's theme was Under the Sea, and Chelsea and I had each worn eight octopus arms. Mostly because we thought announcing to everyone, in an alien voice, that we were a "pair of octopodes" was hilarious. No one else seemed to think it was that funny, but we'd literally double over with laughter every time we said it. So it was totally worth it. Also, dancing together with sixteen arms was the bomb.

"When's the dance again?" Chelsea asks.

"February." Trina pushes the idea jar our way.

"What table are you two at?"

"Oh, Rahul's at Mathletes," Chelsea answers, making me wince ever so slightly. "And I'm trying to get people to sign up for the International Bazaar."

"The International Bazaar? Oh!" Trina gasps. "Is that what those ladies in those awesome dresses were talking about in assembly?"

"Mm-hmm."

"What can you sign up for?"

"Anything really. Setup. Breakdown. Be in the show."

"Well, we better go!" I say, tugging on Chelsea's sleeve before she can do any more promoting. "I promised David I was getting us cookies."

We keep making our way to the musical table.

"I forgot about Sadie Hawkins," I say. Then I do my best alien voice. "How will we ever top octopodes?"

I'm expecting Chelsea to laugh, but instead she says, "Hey, Ra, do you think maybe this year we should go with other people to the dance?"

"You mean, like, in a group? With who?"

"No. I mean. You know. Like"—she hesitates—"should we ask someone?"

"What do you mean, 'ask someone'?"

"You know. Like a date."

"A date?" I suppress a laugh. But when I look at Chelsea, she's just chewing on her fingernail. "Why would we want to do that?"

"Well, I don't know. But, like, what if someone asks you?"

"No one's going to ask me." I shake my head.

"You don't know that. And besides, just because it's 'girls ask guys' doesn't mean you couldn't ask someone yourself. I mean, if you wanted to."

"Who would I want to ask?" This whole conversation is making me uncomfortable. Then it dawns on me. "Wait. Is this why you wanted to know who was at the Mathletes table? Do you wanna go with *David*?"

"No!" She waves her hands in the air. "I mean, maybe. I don't know. Just forget it!"

We snag as many cookies as we can without Mrs. Daugherty noticing, and then I make my way back to the Mathletes booth.

"There you are!" David paws at his throat like he hasn't eaten for days. "Need. Cookies. Now. What took you so long?"

"Sorry. Sorry," I say. "I ran into Chelsea."

I search his face to see if there's any reaction to

her name. But he just grabs the cookie out of my hand, saying, "Sweet!" And then I'm distracted by Gina sliding her chair out and leaning across the table with a clipboard.

"Do you want to join the Mathletes?" she asks.

I turn to see Jai Parikh there. Super-tall Jai Parikh. Running two fingers back and forth across the wispy little hairs on his upper lip.

"It's not too late?" he asks.

Great. Just great. The *other* nerdy Indian is joining.

I look to see if Brent notices, but he's still standing on the wrestling table, his head buried in his arm. He's kissing his bicep.

CHAPTER 26

The last few weeks before winter break, I hole myself up in my bedroom every day after school, surrounded by a flurry of practice tests. It turns out, I have a lot to catch up on with Mathletes. The Mathletics competition covers sixth-, seventh- *and* eighth-grade math, and I've already missed several after-school team meetings.

Bhai has to page me over the walkie-talkies one night. "Hey, Rahul! Even Ramanujan needed a dinner break!" He acts all stern, but I can tell he's proud.

Every week, Mr. Hayden emails us problem sets to work on at home. Timed drills with only a minute to solve each problem. Long-form tests with more complicated problems, where showing your work is key. And twice a week, we practice after school as a team in Mr. Hayden's classroom.

It's hard. Way harder than the math we do in class.

But it's worth it.

Our school has never gone to states.

Yet.

And then, finally, just in time for the first snow of the year, winter break starts. Mr. Hayden says we all deserve a rest. "Get out of here! Go sledding! Stuff your faces and stay up late!"

And even though I beg him to give me a few extra practice tests to take home, today, all those practice tests will have to wait.

Because today is my second-favorite day of the entire year.

Second only to Diwali.

Christmas is only a few days away, and *today* is the day we go Christmas shopping.

Which means we all pile into Mom's minivan and

go to the mall. Even Chelsea comes. Chelsea, Arun, and I get to wander around the mall while Mom, Dad, and Bhai shop for presents to, as Mom tells Arun, "supplement the presents from the North Pole."

We have to swear not to peek in the bags when they load them into the back of the van. Then for dinner we all go to Pizza Hut!

Greenville Mall isn't exactly the Mall of America or anything. You can pretty much see from one end of it to the other. But at Christmas, the whole place is lit up with twinkling white lights, and blankets of cotton are stretched out over everything to look like snow. Giant holiday wreaths and glittery snowflakes line the store entrances, and there's a towering Christmas tree with decorations the size of Arun's head in the center of it all. It reaches almost all the way to the top of the second story.

Chelsea and I are shoving our hands into giant bags of caramel popcorn from Doc Popcorn, and Arun's face is streaked with cinnamon sugar from an Auntie Anne's pretzel as we glide down the escalator, gazing at the tree.

Arun points at the SantaLand next to the Christmas tree and mumbles, "Uh wunna meet Sanba!" His mouth is full of sugary dough.

Chelsea and I roll our eyes, but on days like this, even Arun doesn't get us down.

"Okay, Rooney." Chelsea tousles his hair, leaving bits of popcorn all over his head.

The line to meet Santa is ginormous. Parents nudge oversize shopping bags along the floor in front of them with their toes as the line slowly snakes forward. Kids Arun's age bounce up and down impatiently like they might pee themselves before they make it to the front.

Chelsea's just about to go toss our popcorn bags in the trash when a finger jabs my collarbone. "Oh, hey, Rahul, thanks for saving our place in line."

I look up to see Brent and a seven-year-old female version of Brent trying to push their way in front of us. My stomach sinks.

"What's that?" Chelsea asks.

Brent covers the side of his mouth with one hand and whispers, "Just act like we're together. This line's too long and my dad's making me take this brat to meet Santa. As soon as I'm done with this I get to go to GameStop."

Brent's sister slurps on a swirly-rainbow lollipop the size of a pumpkin.

"I don't think so." Chelsea steps forward, closing

the gap between us and the mom buried in her cell phone in front of us.

"Just be cool. What's it matter to you?"

"We waited just like everyone else. Why should you get special treatment?"

"Fine, I'll get in *behind* you! Just let me in." Brent's not even bothering to whisper anymore, and the dad behind us glares at him.

"That's not the point! You have to wait like everyone else," Chelsea says. I wrap my arm protectively around Arun's shoulder.

"Why are you guys even in this line?" The vein in Brent's neck is bulging.

"We're taking my brother to meet Santa," I say, and Brent turns to look me in the eye.

"My point exactly. Why?"

I'm not sure what he means, but I feel a rising dread.

"Your people shouldn't even be celebrating Christmas," Brent says. "So why are you here?"

"Excuse me?!" Chelsea cuts in.

Brent keeps his eyes fixed on me. "I'm talking to Rahul. Not you."

Arun's face is total shock, and I am flooded with

anger. I've never hated Brent more than I do right at this moment. For as long as I can remember, Christmas has meant vacation and playing in the snow and time with Mom and Dad and getting to go to the mall and staying up all night waiting for presents and watching movies with Bhai and everything *good.*

And I know all *my people* are not Christian, but some of them are. And for the ones who aren't, living in America has made celebrating Christmas a tradition. I bet if Brent's family lived in India, they'd start celebrating Diwali.

"Do you even believe in Santa Claus?" Brent's almost yelling at me now.

"Oh, I'm sorry!" Chelsea screams back at him. "Are you saying that you're in the seventh grade and you *still* believe in *SANTA CLAUS*?"

Parents around us are covering their kids' ears now, and Brent's sister's face looks as horrified as Arun's.

Brent sputters, realizing his mistake. "Well, I mean . . . NO! I mean, duh. That's not what I meant."

His sister pulls on the leg of his jeans. "Why don't you believe in Santa Claus?" she asks in the teensiest voice I've ever heard. Arun's eyes are the size of dinner plates.

And then, without any warning, Brent's sister begins to wail so hard that her entire body convulses. Fountains of water burst out of her eyes.

The dad behind us butts in, "Where are your parents?"

"I'm right here." Brent's dad strides in behind Brent. "What did you do to your sister? I can hear her halfway down the mall!"

"Nothing." Brent actually looks scared for once. "I was just—"

"I asked you to watch her for five minutes!" Mr. Mason fumes. "Can't you even do that? Come on, we're going home."

"What about GameStop?" Brent asks, and I'm surprised he has the courage.

"Are you kidding me? Let's go. NOW!"

Arun tugs on my sweater as they walk away. "Let's get more pretzels. I don't want to do this anymore."

And even though Mom had told us we could each buy only one sweet treat, Chelsea and I take Arun back to Auntie Anne's. We buy a large cup of Cinnamon Sugar Pretzel Nuggets and sit on a bench on the second floor, digging our hands in the bottom of the cup as we watch the crowds of shoppers below us. The line to SantaLand slowly trudges along while we wait for Mom, Dad, and Bhai.

When they finally come get us, none of us even tries to peek in the shopping bags.

CHAPTER 27

Mr. Hayden hangs his head, his shirtsleeves rolled up and his palms pressed firmly into his desk. "Come on! I know you guys can do this. Anyone have any ideas?"

Jenny, Gina, David, Jai, and I are huddled around a table in Mr. Hayden's room. Outside the windows, the sun has already set, and the air looks like a dark black mass of nothingness.

"The district match is tomorrow." Mr. Hayden taps the desk with his fingers. "Work as a team! Brainstorm. Anything. The clock is ticking."

"Okay," Jenny starts in. "Gina, remember last year when we'd get stuck? Everyone on the team would—"

"We didn't win last year," Gina says, cutting her off. "Clearly, *last* year didn't work."

David crumples up yet another piece of paper, tossing it into the growing heap of trash on the floor. "I know," he says. "Maybe we should take a break. Think about something else for a second. And then come back to it fresh."

"What?" Jenny's cheeks grow red. "We don't have time to *take a break*!"

"She's right," Jai says.

"Let's stay focused!" Mr. Hayden jumps in. "Work together. Working as a team is the way to beat Prairieville tomorrow."

I press my thumbs against my temples, and the display of certificates and ribbons taunts me from the opposite wall.

We can't mess this up.

I read the problem on the whiteboard silently to myself.

A ROBOTIC CODE . . .

NINE NUMBERS GROUPED INTO SETS OF THREE BASED ON THE FOLLOWING RULES . . .

ONE NUMBER IN EACH SET IS DESIGNATED AS A KEY.

IF THE NINE NUMBERS ARE . . .

WHAT IS THE PRODUCT OF THE THREE NUMBERS?

"Wait, wait, wait," I say, holding up my hand. "We just need to figure out the third key. Once we know that, it'll all fall into place."

"Right." Jenny nods, catching on. "Because we know there's only one key in each set."

"Okay," Jai says. "The rules say nine and eleven can be in any of the sets—"

"You mean seven and eleven," I correct him.

"No, I don't," he says, and I can hear the defensiveness in his voice. "I mean nine and eleven."

"Sorry to break it to you, Jai," Gina says, writing down the numbers in her notebook, "but Rahul's right. We also know eighteen, thirty-six, and forty-two have to be in different sets."

"But we know it can't be eighteen." Jenny reaches across the table to draw an X through the eighteen in Gina's notebook. "Because that would break the rules."

"Watch it." Gina pushes her arm away. "Use your own notebook."

"Kids!" Mr. Hayden claps his hands together. "What's with all the squabbling today?"

"Sorry," Gina mumbles.

We each work quietly in our own notebooks for a minute.

"So I think our three numbers are seven, thirty-six, and eleven," Jai says.

"I got the same thing!" I say. "But let's double-check."

"If you both got the same thing, doesn't that count as double-checking?" David asks.

"I guess." I bite the back of my pencil. "But let's just make sure it fits all the rules."

"Twenty seconds, guys." Mr. Hayden hovers over our table.

"It works out," I say excitedly. "We got it! It's seven, thirty-six, and eleven."

"Time!" Mr. Hayden calls.

We all high-five.

Everyone *except* Mr. Hayden.

"That's not quite right," he says. "Yes, the set *is* seven, thirty-six, and eleven, but the question was, 'What is the *product* of the three numbers?' So to get credit for the answer, you have to multiply those numbers together to get—"

I quickly do the math in my head. "It's 2,772! Shoot!" I pound my fist on the table. Ugh. What a dumb mistake!

"All right, don't beat yourself up." Mr. Hayden puts his hand on the back of my chair. "But remember. To beat Prairieville, you need to pay attention. Now, let's pack it up. Everyone will be competing in the Individuals Competition tomorrow. For the Team Competition it will be Jai, Jenny, Gina, and Rahul. Now get some sleep. School van leaves the parking lot at six thirty a.m. And don't forget to wear your team T-shirts!"

We tumble out of the room and say our goodbyes. As we head our separate ways to our lockers, David falls in step with me.

"Hey, nice work back there."

"I guess," I say. "But if it were the actual test, we would have missed that one."

"Well, hopefully tomorrow goes better, right?"

"Yeah." It *has* to go better tomorrow.

"Oh, hey," he says, "did Chelsea tell you we thought of a costume for Sadie Hawkins next Friday?"

After winter break, Chelsea actually did it. The second week back to school, at morning assembly, a giggly Trina announced, "The theme of this year's Sadie Hawkins dance is Dynamic Duos!" That very day, Chelsea worked up the courage to go to David's locker and ask him to be her date.

"So, what's the costume?" I ask.

"Oh." He grazes the toe of his sneaker along the floor. "Well, if she didn't tell you, maybe I shouldn't say. She might want it to be a surprise."

"Okay." I shrug. But I don't want to think about Sadie Hawkins. Or that I'm not going with Chelsea. Or that she has a secret with David instead of me.

Or that it's a week away and no girl has asked me yet.

I just want to win tomorrow.

CHAPTER 28

That night, all I can think about is beating Prairieville. Every time I start to doze off, a sea of numbers floods my brain and panic starts to set in. I get out of bed and triple-check to make sure I have all my pencils and erasers in my backpack. But the panic doesn't go away. Finally, I tiptoe down our creaky stairs to check the lock on the front door. Then I make my way to the kitchen. It's so dark, I have to crouch down in front of the stove just to make out the word *off* on each of the five dials. "Off, off, off, off, off," I whisper to myself. Then I walk over to the sink, and I run my hand under the kitchen faucet five times. It's off.

When I get back to my room, I crawl on my knees beside my bed and reach my hand between the outlet on the wall and my bed skirt. I wave it five times. Then I press the button on my alarm clock that reveals what time the alarm is set for. "Five thirty a.m., five thirty a.m., five thirty a.m., five thirty a.m., five thirty a.m.," I whisper.

And then, after what seems like forever, but also way too soon, my alarm actually goes off, and it's morning.

I get out of bed and head downstairs. The only light on in the kitchen is the one hanging over the table, and the room is filled with shadows. Mom's setting out cereal and cutting a banana. I expect her to be the only one up, but Bhai's there too, bundled up with an extra blanket on his lap and a mug of steaming chai in his hands.

"Eat quickly. We should leave just after six," Mom says. "I'm going to shower." Then she leaves us alone.

"Feeling good, Rahulanujan?" Bhai smiles.

I crack a small smile back. "When'd you think of that name?"

"Let's just say you're not the only one with brains in the family." He taps his head. "So? How do you feel?"

"Okay."

But I'm tired. I'm more tired than I can tell him. And I'm nervous, too.

The school van pulls up to Summit Middle School, and Mr. Hayden offers his hand to each of us as we pile out into the parking lot one by one. I step over a clump of dirt-covered snow and pull my hat down over my head. Groups of students follow the neon poster boards directing "Mathletics This Way↑."

"Everyone ready?" Mr. Hayden pulls the van door shut behind us. I watch as he locks it.

Today's the day Mr. Hayden's been waiting for his whole teaching career. Never in the history of Greenville Junior High has he had a team win districts. It's not that he hasn't had smart kids. He's had *very* smart kids. He has tons of certificates and ribbons to prove it.

But none of them has ever been able to win districts and advance to states.

Ever.

And only the top two Individuals winners and the top Team winner today will get to do that.

I exhale, and my breath forms a cloud in the cold air.

A group of kids with Prairieville Middle School written on their team T-shirts walks by. Their coach raises her hand in our direction. "Hayden! Glad you're here again! May the best team win!"

I kick the pinecone-sized pile of ice at my feet. So that's Prairieville.

I swallow, and my breakfast almost comes up in my throat.

We head into the Summit gym, where the Individuals Competition will take place. The gym is filled with rows of long folding tables, two chairs at each one. Monitors walk up and down the aisles, making sure tests stay facedown until it's time to begin.

I walk through the crowds of kids looking for my assigned seat. When I find it, I turn to look for the rest of my team, but I can't find them. It's just a sea of faces.

I start setting up. I lay out one, two, three, four, five mechanical pencils. All brand-new. All with erasers. Plus one extra-large eraser. Just in case.

The kid sitting at my table smirks. "Got enough pencils there?"

I shrug. I tell myself to just stay in the zone. I hold my breath, waiting.

"Begin!" a voice calls through the speaker system. I flip my test over.

The first few questions aren't hard. At all. A fraction here, some integers there, pretty basic formulas. I smile and chew on the inside of my lip. I've got this. I'm way ahead of the game, entering into the last five problems. I still have ten whole minutes left to go.

To my surprise, my mechanical pencil runs out of lead on question twenty-eight. I shake it, and the kid next to me looks my way. I shoot him an "I told you so" look and grab a new one.

Question twenty-nine is a three-part problem. A) How fast are Zack and Zeke traveling up and down a hill? B) What time do they meet? And C) How far from the top and the bottom are they when they meet?

I'm halfway through the third part when something doesn't seem right. My distances don't add up. How can that be? I'm good at these kinds of problems.

I quickly scan my work.

"Two minutes until all pencils are down," the moderator calls out.

Wait, what? I haven't even started question thirty. I look at it.

Ugh.

It's so complicated. Eight kids—all with names that start with a *J*—are playing wizards, goblins, and sorcerers. How many kids end up being wizards?

Oh, come on. Is this a math test or a Harry Potter movie?

"One minute."

I'll just have to skip thirty. Cut my losses.

I go back to question twenty-nine. I must have made an error on part A, I tell myself.

I did. Zack is only averaging *three* miles an hour!

"Ten seconds."

It's 880 yards. They're 880 yards from the top and 430 yards from the bottom. I scratch my answer in.

"Pencils down!"

I flip my test over and slide down my chair in exhaustion. A monitor picks up my test just as two kids from Prairieville walk by.

"Did you finish?" one asks the other.

"You know it! Answered all thirty! Slam dunk!"

My jaw drops. How is that possible? I didn't even get to the last question. Did *everybody* answer all thirty?

The lunchroom at Summit is so much smaller than the one at Greenville, but Mr. Hayden already has a table scoped out for us. We each grab a boxed lunch and make our way over.

"Well!? Individuals Competition down!" He beckons us to hurry up. "You all ready for Team? How'd everyone do?"

"Fine," Gina says, unwrapping her peanut butter and jelly sandwich.

I take a bite of mine, but as I chew on it, my stomach turns inside out. Like swallowing might make me throw up.

"You guys think we can take down Prairieville?" Mr. Hayden's eyes gleam with expectation.

I bury my face behind the lid of the box and spit out my sandwich.

"Everything okay, Rahul?" Mr. Hayden asks.

I feel a tear pooling in my eye and fight it back. "I didn't finish the test."

Five heads stop midbite and turn my way.

Mr. Hayden tries to hide it, but I can hear the disappointment in his voice. "Well, that's okay. How did you feel about the ones you did finish?"

"Fine." I keep my head down. "I took the time to double-check everything, and I'm pretty sure all my other answers were right."

I can't bring myself to look at him.

"And how many did you answer?"

"Twenty-nine."

For a second, no one moves.

Then Mr. Hayden breaks into a huge grin. "Rahul! If you got twenty-nine out of thirty questions right, you're in excellent shape!"

I look out at the cafeteria, swarming with kids from all over the region.

I mumble, "I bet someone in here got all thirty."

"Maybe not." Jenny puts her hand on my arm. "It was super hard. I answered all of them, but I definitely didn't have time to double-check. I'm pretty sure I got a couple wrong."

I shrug. "Yeah, well, one of the Prairieville kids answered all thirty. I heard him talking about it. And *he* probably double-checked."

"Duuuude." David crosses his arms behind his head. "You gotta ease up! I didn't even bother with the last three. They were way too hard!"

Gina laughs into her half-eaten sandwich.

I want to tell her to knock it off. I want to tell Jenny that it's irresponsible not to double-check your work, and I want to tell David that no one's expecting him to win anyway. But I don't know why I feel so angry at them. They're my team.

So, instead, I wipe my hands on the front of my jeans and stand up, pushing my chair out with my shaky legs.

"Whatever. Let's go win Teams!"

The Team Competition takes place in several classrooms, so that the groups can spread out and actually talk to each other without being overheard. Jai, Jenny, Gina, and I walk into classroom 2B. We're headed toward our table when we hear a sarcastic "Ooh, which one of you nerds thought of those hilarious T-shirts?"

We stop in front of the team from Creston Middle, settling into their chairs.

"I said, which one of you nerds thought of those hilarious T-shirts?" the kid repeats.

I look down at the front of my maroon shirt, a large "π, anyone?" emblazoned across it in white.

Gina answers, "It's from our teacher's favorite poster." She flips her long brown hair over her shoulder. "Why? You got a problem with it?"

"Yeah," he says, scratching at a scab on his pale, white arm. "It's like *so* original, I can hardly stand it." Then he does some weird accent, like he's trying to make himself sound Indian or something. "Is your teacher as nerdy as you guys?"

"What does that mean?" I say before I realize I'm going to speak. "Besides, it's Mathletics. We're *all* nerds." I remember what Chelsea said in my basement, way back at the beginning of the school year. "That's what makes us fun."

"No." He's relentless. "You guys are like a whole 'nother level. Just look at your team. Two brownies and a Chinese chick."

Jenny takes a step forward. "Get your facts straight. I'm *Japanese American.*"

"And we're Indian. Don't call us brownies," Jai pipes up.

"Yeah, well, why don't you go back to where you belong?" the kid says to Jai. "And take your parents with you before they blow something up."

For a second, I freeze. I can't believe he just said that.

And then I explode. I remember what Mom told me at the bank about standing up for what's right.

"I can't believe how ignorant you are!" I say. "He belongs *right* here! We all do. Just because we're brown doesn't mean we're terrorists. What's wrong with you?"

"Let's go," Gina says. "This guy's a loser." She gets right up in his face. "Maybe you should crawl back into the hole *you* came out of. And never come back."

Luckily, the monitor walks into the room, and we all head to our table.

Maybe it took standing up to that kid from Creston to remind us just how great we can be together. Because suddenly we are the most focused we've ever been. We slide answers on slips of papers across the table. We speak in hushed whispers. We double-check every single problem.

We're a team.

At three p.m. we've finally gathered back in the school gym to find out who the winners are. This is it. The moment of truth. Even Mr. Hayden seems nervous.

I'm pretty sure it's impossible for me to have placed in Individuals. I didn't even finish the test. But I have every finger crossed that maybe, just maybe, we placed as a team.

A teacher from Summit walks up to the mic and taps it with his finger. It feeds back, and hands all over the auditorium fly up to cover ears.

"Sorry about that!" he chuckles. "I'm Mr. Walt Scoky, and I teach eighth-grade mathematics here. Now before we get to handing out the medals, I just want to say what an honor it was for Summit to host the District Mathletics Competition this year."

He pulls a note card out of his pocket, and my heart jumps. Here we go.

"You know, it took a lot of people to put this event together. I just want to be sure to thank all of them."

I rub my hands over my eyes. How long is this going to take?

He thanks, like, a bajillion faculty members, parents for helping in the cafeteria, the kids who printed up all the signs. He might as well be thanking the trees for the paper the signs are printed on.

Finally, he puts the note card back in his pocket. "Listen, kids." He leans into the mic. "This is a competition, but it's so much more than that. You've all done a great job today. You've learned about hard work, you've honed your skills, you've gotten to know yourselves better, you've built camaraderie . . ."

UGH. Will he ever announce the winners?

"You've learned how to work as a team, how to respect one another, and you've learned discipline. So it's not just about who wins."

Of course it's about who wins! It's a competition!

"So, without further ado, let's begin." He flips over a new note card. "For the team winners. In third place, let's give a huge congratulations to the fine kids at Briarwood Middle School!"

A group of students lets out a cheer as the team from Briarwood makes their way down the bleachers. My stomach is tied up in a million knots.

"Now, it was very close between our second- and first-place teams. And, remember, the first-place team will be advancing to the Indiana State Mathletics Competition!"

WE KNOW! JUST SAY WHO WON!

"Second place goes to . . ." He pauses. He closes his eyes and leans his head back for so long that the entire room goes still.

Then he snaps his head forward and sneezes. Right into the microphone. Hundreds of hands fly up to cover our ears again.

"Excuse me! Sorry about that. I must be allergic to all the talent in here!"

He digs around in his back pocket. "I think I have a handkerchief somewhere here."

I can't even stay seated anymore. Literally. My butt is hovering two inches above the bleachers.

He blows his nose. "Alrighty, then . . . second place goes to . . . Prairieville Middle School!"

Wait.

PRAIRIEVILLE GOT SECOND? They were the team to beat.

Could that mean?

No, no, no. It would be too good to be true. There's no way we beat Prairieville.

I look over at Mr. Hayden. His fingers are crossed on both hands.

The kids from Prairieville are on the gym floor now, shaking Mr. Scoky's hand. They're nodding and patting each other on the back, but you can see the disappointment in their faces.

"And now, for the team that will represent our

district at the state level . . . the moment you've all been waiting for . . ."

I'm seriously going to start hyperventilating. In a flash, my brain replays every answer to every question in the Team Competition.

"The winner of the District Mathletics Competition is . . ."

My head feels like it's about to explode.

"Greenville Junior High!"

And suddenly all five of us, *and* Mr. Hayden, are jumping up and down so hard that the entire set of bleachers is shaking. We're up in each other's faces, screaming, screaming, screaming nonsense words of joy. I'm bear-hugging David. Gina is racing down the bleachers. Jai is right behind her, one arm on Gina's shoulder and the other fist-bumping the sky.

I can't believe it! We won! My face is frozen in shock.

"Not the humblest group I've ever met." Mr. Scoky smiles as he hands us our medals. "But you all really deserve it."

"Thank you," we mumble as we turn in a daze to head back to our seats.

He pinches the back of my shirt and whispers,

"Don't go all the way back up. You're going to be down here again in just a minute."

Now I really think I might lose it. There's no way I could have won Individuals. I didn't even finish the test. But could I have gotten third place?

Or maybe, just maybe, second?

If I got second, I would still get to compete in Individuals at states.

I take a few steps away, and the whole world goes a little blurry and the sounds in the gym get all echoey in my head. I see the backs of my classmates as they walk up the stairs, high-fiving kids from other schools along the way. I hear Mr. Scoky announce the third-place Individuals winner, his voice bouncing off the gymnasium walls.

It isn't my name he calls. Does this mean maybe, just maybe, I got second?

A bunch of kids start whooping and hollering as the third-place winner bounds down the bleachers two steps at a time. Mr. Scoky hands him a bronze medal.

And then the world snaps back into real time.

"Second place in Individuals goes to . . ."

I let out a slow breath.

"James Wright, from Prairieville Middle School!"

I bury my face in my hands, and now I'm full-on crying.

I can't believe it.

"Our first-place winner is Rahul Kapoor, from Greenville Junior High!"

CHAPTER 29

By the time we get back to the van, the sun has dipped into a golden-pink line on the edge of the horizon.

Mr. Hayden spins around in the front seat as he starts the car. “I am so proud of you guys right now. All of you. Just wait until Principal Jacobson hears we’re going to states. Both the team *and* Rahul!”

I don’t know if it’s the sheer exhaustion from getting up in the middle of the night to check all the locks and appliances, or maybe it’s the fact that I haven’t eaten since breakfast. Or maybe it’s just the adrenaline from the day. But at some point on the ride home, the gentle rocking of the van lulls me into a deep sleep.

When I wake up, it's pitch-black outside except for the occasional headlight from oncoming traffic. I look up from the last row of the van, and it seems like everyone else is dozing too. Except for Mr. Hayden, of course, who has two hands on the steering wheel, his eyes steady on the road.

I'm not sure what woke me up, so I close my eyes to settle back into my nap, when I feel a warm breath against my neck.

"Rahul?"

I nearly choke myself on my seat belt.

It's Jenny. She's poking me in the arm.

"What?" I ask, my voice all crackly from the dry air.

"Quiet," she says. "Everyone's sleeping."

She's crawled across the row so that she's sitting right next to me.

"You should be in your seat," I whisper. "With your seat belt on."

"I know. But . . ." She hesitates and I catch a faint whiff of our boxed lunches on her breath. Peanut butter. "I just wanted to talk to you."

"Okay. What's up?"

"You were awesome today."

"Thanks. You too."

"And it was cool how you stood up to that Creston kid."

"Oh. Well, you too," I say.

A pair of headlights passes by the window and an orange-yellow glow flickers across Jenny's face. We smile at each other.

"Can I ask you a question?" she says.

"Yeah."

"Do you want to . . . um."

I swivel in my seat to see her better, and I can tell that her face looks anxious.

"Do you want to . . . ," she starts again.

"Do I want to . . . what?"

But she still doesn't say anything, so I ask again, "What is it?"

She exhales. "Okay. Okay. I was just . . . um. Will you go to Sadie Hawkins with me this Friday?"

Another set of headlights goes by, and this time her eyes are shining.

For a second I consider pretending that she didn't say anything at all. Ever since Chelsea asked David, I've been hoping someone would ask me. But now that it's here . . .

“Why does your face look like that?” she asks. “Is that a no?”

“No!” I whisper-shout.

“It *is* a no?” She looks like she might cry.

“No. No, it’s not a no!”

“So, it’s a—”

I jump back in. “It’s not a yes either. I mean, yet. I mean . . .” Shoot, shoot, shoot. I scramble for what to say, “It’s a . . . I mean . . . it’s just that I have to ask my parents. That’s all.”

A smile forms along the edges of her lips. “So if they say yes, does that mean you’ll go with me?”

“Yes.”

And then her hand brushes against mine as she drags herself back to her seat. And I think I should feel excited.

So why do I feel scared?

CHAPTER 30

I must have been way more tired than I thought, because on Sunday morning, I'm still in bed when I hear the familiar sounds of my favorite Bollywood song, "Yeh Dosti Hum Nahi Todenge," reverberating through our whole house.

Is that Bollywood Supply? Why are they playing Bhai's and my song? I pop up in the bed and fling my covers off. And what time is it? I turn over to look at my alarm clock.

Twelve fifteen?! It's after *noon*?

I fly down the stairs in my pajamas, my hair standing up every which way. As soon as I get to the kitchen, I run into a wall of neon green and red.

"Hi, Rahul beta!" The wall is Nandita Auntie's sari. "Come, come. Sit down."

The Auntie Squad has taken over the kitchen. Again.

I pull out a chair, and Nandita Auntie slides a plate in front of me.

"Nice of you to join us, sleepyhead," Arun says from across the table, where Juhi Auntie is hand feeding him pieces of potato *pakoras*.

"Morning, Rahul." Mom walks around the table and kisses my head. "I was just telling the aunties about your big win!" She heads back over to the easel set up in front of the kitchen counter. It says "Advertise the Bazaar at" on top, and below that are a bunch of bullet points:

- THE MALL
- LOCAL BUSINESSES
- GREENVILLE COMMUNITY COLLEGE
- SCHOOLS
- CHURCHES/TEMPLES

"Did you all see his medal?" Moms asks the room.

"Did I see it?" Nandita Auntie slides a heaping

plate of food under my nose. "I'm so proud, I'm wearing it as my jewelry from now on!"

The rest of the aunties burst into laughter, and I notice my first-place gold medal sitting on the kitchen table. Mom must have snuck it out of my room to show everyone while I was still sleeping. I try not to smile too hard.

Bollywood Supply strikes a final chord, and the door to the garage flies open.

"Ladies," Vinay Uncle calls out, popping his head into the doorframe. "Is it safe for the men to enter? We just want a glass of water."

Urvi Auntie flings a piece of raw dough at his face, and he ducks just in time. "Enter at your own risk!" she shrieks, and the Squad erupts all over again.

Jeet Uncle picks up the dough as Dad swoops in and kisses Mom on the cheek.

"How's Bazaar planning going?" Dad asks, turning on the faucet and filling up glasses of water in the sink.

"Excellent!" Mom says. "Now that Juhi's found a football field for us, we're doubling down on getting the word out. I want to pack that place."

Urvi Auntie points to two oversize cardboard

boxes filled with photocopied flyers. "We're putting these all over town. Everyone will know about the Bazaar!"

Vinay Uncle reaches across the table to pick up my medal. "What's this?" he asks.

Dad beams with pride. "My son is going to the State Math Competition! He won first place in the entire region yesterday. Can you believe it?" He hands Vinay Uncle a glass of water. "He's a gold medalist!"

Vinay Uncle purses his lips. "Well. It's good, but let's not get carried away. It's not like he won the Olympics." He puts the medal back down and gingerly wipes his hand on the front of his pants. Like my medal might give him the cooties or something.

Dad looks at Vinay Uncle and his eyes narrow ever so slightly. "Well, if you ask me, it is like he won the Olympics." His voice is surprisingly firm. "He's the first person from his school to *ever* go to states. That's a big deal. In fact, the whole team won first place, too."

Everyone waits for Vinay Uncle to react, but he doesn't say anything. I see Mom quietly smiling at Dad.

Then she claps her hand to her forehead. "Oh! I almost forgot. Speaking of your team. Rahul, Mrs.

Ikeda called me this morning. She said Jenny asked you to the school dance?"

"*Jenny?*" Nandita Auntie shrieks. "Who is this *Jenny*? You're taking her to a dance?"

"Well, I—" I try to get a word in edgewise. But it's impossible. Nandita Auntie's on a roll.

"I didn't know there was a *Jenny*! You have *two* girlfriends now? Does Chelsea know?"

Mom goes on, "Mrs. Ikeda said you told Jenny you wanted to go, but you needed my permission. So I told her it's fine. She wants you to call. Something about making a costume."

"You told Jenny you needed your mom's permission?" Nandita Auntie reaches over and pinches my cheeks. "What about your auntie's permission? Now I don't know whose wedding to plan! Chelsea's? Jenny's? Chelsea's *and* Jenny's?"

"I better go." I jump out of my chair. All I want to do is get out of this room. But before I leave, I say loud enough to make sure Vinay Uncle hears, "I don't want to keep my date waiting!"

When I get upstairs, I take Mom's cell phone and dial Mrs. Ikeda's number.

"Hi. Is Jenny there? This is Rahul."

There's a rustling noise, and then Jenny gets on the phone.

"Hi, Rahul." Jenny immediately launches into an apology. "I am *so* sorry my mom called. I *told* her not to do that. But she was like—he already said yes! Let me just confirm it's okay!"

"It's all right," I say. "So, the theme is Dynamic Duos, right? What do you want to go as?" For a second, the dance seems like it could actually be fun. Maybe even a lot of fun.

"Well, I was thinking," Jenny says, "now that we won districts and all, that we should go as something math related." She pauses. "Except I'm not sure about the 'duo' part." She pauses again. "Or the 'dynamic' part."

I laugh, and she laughs back. But somehow, the fact that we're laughing together makes the dance start to seem so real.

I'm going to have to dance with Jenny. Like, put my arms around her. What if I do it wrong? How am I even *supposed* to do it? If I do it wrong, will people think that I'm . . . ?

"So, in any case," she says, "I think we could just make our own costumes. Do you want to come over to my place? Like today, and figure it out? My mom said she could pick you up. We have a bunch of old cardboard boxes in the garage. I'm sure we could come up with something."

I don't say anything.

"Rahul? You still there?"

I run my hand along the cord of my alarm clock. "Um, I'll go as whatever, but I can't come over today."

There's a silence on the phone line. Then she says, "Okay. No problem. I'll get my mom and dad to help."

I still don't say anything.

"It's going to be so fun, Rahul."

"Yeah, totally," I say quietly.

CHAPTER 31

It's the day of the Sadie Hawkins dance. It's also the day Principal Jacobson is going to announce at morning assembly that the math team is going to states.

It's not like half the school doesn't already know we won. Mr. Hayden has been broadcasting it to all his classes. For an entire week now, the top of his whiteboard has been emblazoned with a block-lettered "WE'RE GOING TO STATES!!!" in multicolored marker.

It's more like most people don't seem to care.

I guess I thought being the best at something would make things different.

All week long, I've been carrying my medal in my backpack, carefully wrapped in the padded laptop section of my bag to protect it from scratches.

On Monday, in the car to school, I showed it to Chelsea.

"This is so cool!" Chelsea said, her fingers tracing the embossed "1st Place" on the front of it. "I knew you could do it!"

So, at least *she* cares.

And I know Principal Jacobson cares. According to Mr. Hayden, she saved announcing it until the day of the Sadie Hawkins dance so that the whole night would be a kind of celebration for us.

Which is why I'm beyond nervous as she calls the entire middle school to order.

"Good morning, everyone!" Principal Jacobson double-taps the edge of her papers on the podium. "As you all know, tonight is the Sadie Hawkins dance. I hope you're all planning to attend.

"Now the tradition of Sadie Hawkins, ironically, is to buck tradition. There's no need for girls to have to wait around for boys to ask them to a dance. Girls can feel empowered to make the first move, too."

A bunch of students giggle when she says "first move." Next to me, Chelsea rolls her eyes. I look over my shoulder, and from three rows back, I see Jenny smiling at me.

"But you also don't need a date to come, and really, anyone can ask anyone. We just hope you'll all be there tonight."

"Can boys ask boys?" someone in the back yells in a disguised voice, dragging out their *s*'s. There's another round of giggling, and a flash of heat climbs up my neck and into my ears.

"Anyone can ask anyone," Principal Jacobson repeats. "Look, I know you're all excited about the dance tonight, but that's no excuse for all this unruliness. Now, tonight, while we're all dancing our feet off, we'll also be celebrating a huge achievement in the history of Greenville Junior High."

Here it comes. Chelsea reaches over and wraps her fingers around my arm.

"When Mr. Hayden joined the faculty over a decade ago, he enrolled Greenville in the annual Mathletics competition. As you all know, it only takes a brief visit to Mr. Hayden's classroom to see how successful he's been. Over the last ten years, his Mathletes have brought home more ribbons and certificates than I can count. Although I bet every one of his Mathletes could add it up really fast!"

A few people chuckle, and someone yells out, "Pi, anyone?"

"But in those ten years," Principal Jacobson goes on, "there has been one honor that has eluded these talented teams. I'd like to ask Mr. Hayden, Gina Carvallo, Jenny Ikeda, Rahul Kapoor, David Nguyen, and Jai Parikh up to the stage."

Chelsea and I do a quick BRiC as I head toward the podium. Mr. Hayden's already there, proudly holding our districts trophy in one hand.

"These bright young Greenville students . . ."

"Nerds!" someone yells out.

"These bright young Greenville students," Principal Jacobson continues, undeterred, "have, for the first time in our school's history, won first place at districts. I am proud to say that the team will be taking our school to the State Mathletics Competition!"

There is a smattering of applause, but I have to be honest—I thought there'd be more.

"And on top of that," Principal Jacobson says, smiling in my direction, "Rahul Kapoor placed first out of everyone in the entire competition. So he will also be going to states as an Individuals competitor, which could qualify him to go to the national competition in Washington, DC."

There's a little more applause and some genuine hushed aahs of appreciation.

Then, I see Chelsea stand up in her seat and yell out, "Way to go, Mathletes!" I bite my lip to suppress my smile.

And then, the strangest thing. A few kids behind her stand up, too, and start clapping.

And then a few more.

And then, in the cool-kids' section, I see Justin stand up. He sticks two fingers in his mouth and whistles. Chelsea glances over her shoulder at him, and then she starts chanting, "Math-letes! Math-letes!"

And then one by one, the entire middle school starts to stand.

My heart flies up into my throat as the room thunders with "Math-letes! Math-letes! Math-letes!"

If this standing ovation never ends, I'd be totally fine with it.

The gym is decked out with silver streamers and rainbow-colored balloons for the Sadie Hawkins dance. The walls have been plastered with glitter letters spelling out "Dynamic Duos!" "Two Peas in a Pod!" and "Can't Have One without the Other!"

Someone's even taped up a hand-drawn poster that says, "Congratulations, Mathletes!" It looks like it was made last-minute, but it's there. Mrs. Daugherty is doing the snake behind the DJ booth, and I spot Mr. Hayden handing out punch at the snack table.

I brace myself as Jenny and I walk in. But to my surprise, a few people actually head over to congratulate us on our win. Trina and her friends even take the time to marvel at our costumes. Jenny's dressed like a giant compass and I'm a human-sized protractor. Her mom and dad spent the whole week helping her make them out of cardboard boxes.

The protractor is strapped to my back with rope and sticks out so far on each side that I have to be careful not to hit anyone in the face. Jenny has a pencil that's almost as tall as she is taped to the side of her compass.

I told her I thought they'd be way too nerdy, but now that we have the Trina Drexel stamp of approval, I feel guilty I didn't help.

We're hovering near the punch table when some guy behind me says, "Toodle-y-oo," in a super high-pitched, fake British accent.

Jenny and I turn around to see Chelsea and David.

"Wait, *what*?" I say. "Who are you guys?"

"Don't you get it?" She spins around proudly. "We're Prince Harry and Meghan Markle!"

"Yeah, but . . ."

Jenny's hand flies over her mouth, and she shrieks as she points at them. She fans her face with both her hands. "David! *Da*vid! I can't believe it!"

I look David up and down.

He's wearing a tiara, lipstick, and a long brown wig. He has a sparkly dress on, and his ankles are wobbling around in high heels.

"Cool, right?" Chelsea says, tilting her orange-wigged head and tugging on what must be her dad's navy suit blazer. "He's Meghan, and I'm Harry!"

"Wow!" I say, my mouth hanging open. I find myself glancing around the room to see if anyone's looking our way. I sort of can't believe David's okay being dressed like that.

"Oh my gosh!" Chelsea fusses over us. "Your costumes are so perfect!"

"Jenny thought of them. Super smart, right?" I say, trying to smile encouragingly at her.

"Thanks," Jenny says, lowering her eyes. "Rahul looks pretty good, right?"

Her fingers brush against mine like she's trying to hold my hand, and I don't mean to, but I instinctively pull my arm back. Jenny's cheeks redden.

"Um, Ra." Chelsea nudges me. "Isn't there something *you* want to say now?"

I search her face.

Chelsea widens her eyes at me. "You know. Since Jenny said how *good* you look."

"Dude!" David whispers. "You're supposed to say she looks good, too!"

Shame fills my cheeks. "I know. I mean, I already told her!"

"Um, actually, you didn't, but it's fine." Jenny crosses her arms over her chest, making the pencil side and the needle side of her compass slide dangerously far apart. The giant pencil strains against the packing tape.

The rest of the night, Jenny and I mostly sit in the chairs lined up along the edge of the gym, watching everyone else dance. Which in these costumes isn't that easy.

On the dance floor, it seems like Chelsea and David never take a break. David mostly two-steps, his heels in one hand, while Chelsea tears it up. Every time she flies through the air or twirls around, he grabs his forehead with both his hands and laughs like it's the most amazing thing he's ever seen.

"They're pretty funny, huh?" I say.

"Uh-huh," Jenny responds. I'm trying to be nice to her, but I can tell she doesn't want to talk. What did I do wrong?

At one point they play "I Got a Feeling" and the whole gym goes nuts. Besides us, the only people not on the dance floor are the chemistry teacher and Assistant Principal Merriweather. And rumor has it he's 104.

Chelsea comes running over. "No more sitting! You guys *have* to come out for this one!" she screams over the music. "TONIGHT'S THE NIGHT! LET'S LIVE IT UP!" She runs back out, beckoning at us with her waving arms.

"Want to go dance?" I ask Jenny over all the noise.

"You should just go," Jenny says. "Dance with Chelsea if you want. I'm fine to sit."

"You sure?"

She nods yes, but she also clenches her jaw.

"It's okay," I say. "I'll go get us some snacks."

By the time I come back with a plate full of carrots smothered in ranch dressing and crackers topped with spray cheese, the music has shifted to a sappy slow song, and most of the dance floor empties out.

"Carrot?" I offer the plate to Jenny, but she just

sighs and sinks her chin into her fists.

I scan the room for Chelsea, but I don't see her. The only people dancing now are a group of girls singing into air microphones in a circle, and a few awkward couples.

From the DJ booth, Mrs. Daugherty is casting green laser lights across the gym, and one of them lands on Justin and Trina. His arms are resting lightly on her waist. They're dressed like Spider-Man and Mary Jane, and when he does a goofy little kick with his leg to make Trina laugh, I can't help but notice how he looks in his dark blue tights.

I swallow.

Why is everything so confusing?

I'm pretty sure that now that the music has slowed down, I'm supposed to ask Jenny to dance again. Even if she said she didn't want to before. But I feel so scared.

"What's up, Rahul?"

I almost jump out of my seat.

It's Brent, pulling up a chair next to mine.

"Oh, hi." I clear my throat. "What's up?"

He fiddles with the bandanna on his neck. "Just sayin' hi."

I guess he's a cowboy.

"Congrats on your big win," he says.

I drag a carrot through a mound of ranch dressing.

"Pretty cool how Justin stood up for you in convo, huh?"

I shrug.

Brent leans in really close and whispers, "Do you wish you were dancing with him?"

My whole body tenses up.

"I saw you staring at him."

My knee starts to jiggle, and I accidentally knock the plate of food out of my hands.

A glob of ranch dressing lands on the side of Jenny's compass.

"Rahul!" Jenny throws her arms up. "Watch it!"

"Sorry!"

I lean over to pick up the plate, and Brent leans over with me. "Does Jenny know about your secret crush?"

I freeze, my hand wrapped around a carrot, dressing oozing between my fingers.

"What's going on?" Chelsea's voice interrupts us. Brent and I both sit up, nearly knocking heads.

David pops in over her shoulder. "Everything okay?"

"Just helping Rahul clean up his mess," Brent says, making air guns as he walks away.

I want so badly to run out of the gym.

I want to run far, far away and never, ever come back.

Chelsea puts a hand on my shoulder. "Hey, Ra, come with me?"

We're not supposed to be out in the hallways unchaperoned. They're empty and dark. Only the emergency lights are on, and it's hard to see more than four feet in front of us.

We walk in silence down one hallway, through one door to another, and then finally we stop in front of a row of lockers.

"Everything okay?" Chelsea asks.

"Yeah, I guess."

She nudges my arm. "You should be celebrating tonight. Your big win and all. How come you're not dancing?"

I shrug.

"Do you want to talk? What did Brent say to you?"

I open my mouth, but it feels like my throat is

all locked up. I want to say to her that I wouldn't know how to talk about it if I tried. That I don't understand it myself. That I thought winning would change things. But Brent's still being Brent. And I can't stop looking at Justin. And the thought of dancing with Jenny terrifies me. And none of that makes any sense.

"What is it, Ra?" she says, and her voice is so soft it makes me want to cry.

I shake my head and part my lips, but no words come out.

I stare at the floor.

And then finally I say, "Chelsea?" and my voice comes out all scratchy, like when you say something after not having spoken for a long, long time.

"Yeah?"

"I think I might be . . ." My breath comes out, but no words follow.

It seems like an eternity goes by.

"You think you might be . . . ?"

I just keep staring at my feet.

"Would it help if I said it?" she says ever so gently. She hesitates. "Do you think you might be . . . gay?"

Her voice lilts up like a question, but it's like it's a question she already knows the answer to.

Tears start to spill out of my eyes, and I scrunch up my face to try and stop them. But I can't.

I bury my face in my hands, and, somehow, I manage to nod.

"Oh, Ra, it's okay," Chelsea says. She puts an arm on each of my shoulders, and we stand like that for a little while until the tears slow down.

Then I lean into her, and she hugs me tight. "It's really okay."

When I finally look up at her, she says, "Can I ask you something?"

I nod, wiping my cheeks with my hands.

"Do you think you have a crush on Justin?"

My heart sinks into my stomach. "No. I don't know. I don't want to talk about it."

"Okay, sorry."

I sniffle. "Why'd you even ask me that?"

"It's just." She pauses. "Well, sometimes, I see the way you look at him."

Shoot. I know I stare at him sometimes. And I know Brent sees it. But I just thought it was because Brent was always watching me like a hawk. I didn't think anyone else noticed.

I wipe my hand under my nose. "I don't know, Chels. Everything just feels so confusing."

"Confusing how?"

"Just . . ." I don't know how to explain it to her. "Just forget it. I don't want to talk about it."

"You can tell me. Confusing how?"

"Well, sometimes . . ." A wave of embarrassment washes over me. "Sometimes I just wish . . . like, I just wish . . . I *was* him. Justin, I mean."

Chelsea nods, but I can see the question in her eyes.

"Just forget it," I say.

"No, Ra, tell me."

"I mean, like I wish I could be like him. And so . . . I watch him." I shake my head. "To see how to be."

I see even more confusion in Chelsea's face.

"Forget it, let's just go back inside."

"Wait, Ra." She stops me. "Why wouldn't you want to be *you*?"

A few feet away from us, I hear a squeak. Like the sound a sneaker makes when it rubs against a tiled floor. Every hair on the back of my neck sticks straight up into the air.

"What was that?" I whisper.

"I don't know. Is someone there?" Chelsea raises her voice ever so slightly. We both look down the hall, but it's too dark and shadowy to see anything.

Then a door slams.

Silence.

My heart stops in my throat.

"Chelsea, who was that?"

"I don't know, Ra, but whoever it was, I promise it's okay."

"No. It's not! Why did you bring me out here?"

"What do you mean? I just wanted to—"

"I told you we should go back inside!"

"Ra, it's fine."

"No, it's not fine. Chelsea! It's not fine!" Anger fills my whole body. So much anger that I start to shake. "I don't ever want to talk about this again. Not with you. Not with anyone. EVER!"

I run down the hall and fling the door open. "Is anyone there?" I yell.

I'm met with a deafening silence.

I turn back to Chelsea, and my costume gets stuck on the doorjamb. Half of it rips off my back. I scream, "I can't believe you did this!"

And then I run away.

CHAPTER 32

Jai, Jenny, Gina, and I are piled into the school van driving to the State Mathletics Competition with Mr. Hayden. No David this time. He wasn't on the team at districts, so he doesn't advance to states.

This year, the competition is at Purdue University. It's a three-hour drive from Greenville, and, as Mom pointed out, "That's with *zero* traffic!" Since everything starts early in the morning tomorrow, we'll spend the night at a hotel in West Lafayette.

With fewer people in the van, I have the whole back row to myself. Which is fine by me.

I still don't know who heard me in the hallway the night of the dance. Or what they heard. Jenny was sitting exactly where I left her when I got back to the gym, which made me dread that it might have been Brent. But he hasn't said anything to me, and there's no way I'm asking him.

I guess it could have been anyone.

In any case, except for the bare minimum during team practice, Jenny's hardly spoken to me since then.

And Chelsea and I haven't really spoken either.

I don't want to talk to her about what happened in the hallway. But now that it happened, it's like, how do you pretend it didn't?

So we've just stopped talking.

Mr. Wilson called Mom one day to see if she thought Chelsea and I seemed quieter in carpool. Mom asked me if everything was all right, but I just said, "Are you kidding? Me and Chels? Ain't no party like a Rahul and Chelsea party."

At school, I started bringing my math book to lunch and sitting at a table by myself.

On Sundays, when Bhai would ask me when Chelsea was coming over, I'd just say I had math problem sets to work on. No time to play. He'd tell me to come watch a movie when I finished, that too much studying wasn't "healthy." I could see the disappointment in his face when I told him I just didn't have the time.

But it's true. I don't have the time.

I have to win states.

And I don't mean our team. See, if our team wins at states, all we get is a trophy.

What really counts is Individuals.

The top four Individuals winners at states become the team from Indiana to go to nationals.

And if I make it to nationals—I dig my fingers into the seat of the van—I could be named national champion.

I unzip the top pocket of my backpack. One, two, three, four, five mechanical pencils. Check. One eraser. Check. I zip it shut. I open the main pocket. One new notebook. Check. Five practice tests to review. Check. Math book. Check. I rummage around for my calculator and two backup batteries.

Check.

I zip up the pocket. I lean back and look out at the gray sky and the rain streaking across the van window.

Then I unzip the top pocket again. I take out the first pencil. I shake it. Full of lead. Check . . .

Three and a half hours feels like seven, and then finally the van jostles into the hotel parking lot, the tires sloshing through potholes filled with puddles.

It feels more and more like spring every day, and I unzip the top of my windbreaker as we all pile out of the van.

Mr. Hayden gets our keys from the front desk and walks us to our rooms. Jai and I are sharing, and I have to admit, it makes me a little nervous. I've never spent the night in a hotel without my parents.

We call beds and throw our things on the floor. "I'm tired," he says, rifling through his bag. "Wanna watch TV and go to sleep?"

I think about the practice tests waiting in my bag.

"Oh, hey," he's unloading a seemingly endless number of Tupperware containers onto the desk, "my mom packed me some snacks. You want some?"

There's *chevda*, and *farsi puri*, and fried banana chips. And even what looks like homemade samosas. I smile. No one else at our school would *ever* have these.

"Don't be shy," he says. "Or, wait. Do you not like Indian food?" He shoots me a funny look. "Do you even know what these things are?"

"Of course I do!"

"Really?"

"Yeah, why wouldn't I?"

"I don't know. You just—well, you don't seem very Indian."

"What does that mean?" I ask, not sure why I feel slightly offended.

"Nothing, nothing. I didn't mean anything bad. Listen, help yourself, okay?"

I consider telling him how much I love Diwali, and how many Bollywood movies I've seen. But the truth is, I guess I pretty much hide that stuff at school.

He digs around in his bag some more and pulls out a pair of shorts and a T-shirt and starts changing right in front of me.

It's funny, but I realize that I haven't seen any other Indian guys my age, like, changing in front of me. I turn to look away, but for some reason, I don't feel as anxious as I do in the locker room. It's like, seeing him makes me think my body is more okay or something. Like I'm not so different.

"What do you want to watch?" Jai asks as he jumps backward onto his bed.

"You can watch whatever," I say.

I carry my bag into the bathroom and lock the

door behind me. I undress, folding my clothes into a neat stack on the counter next to the little shampoo bottles and white washcloths folded like seashells. I brush my teeth and change into my pajamas. By the time I come back out, Jai's head is tilted to one side, drool running out of the corner of his mouth. The TV is talking to no one.

I walk over to the coffee maker sitting on top of the refrigerator, and I unplug it. I consider unplugging the refrigerator, too, but I worry Jai will notice tomorrow. I turn all the lights off except for the table lamp on the desk. I pull the stack of practice tests out of my bag and get to work, stopping only to eat a samosa.

At six forty-five a.m., we walk up to the mathematics building at Purdue University. Sunlight gleams off the rows of windows sweeping up to the sky. It seems like you could fit a whole country inside here. Kids swarm through the hallways, and the lines at the registration table go on forever.

The auditorium for the Individuals Competition is like a Greek theater. I slide into my assigned seat as a screen scrolls down up front. Projected rules start rolling into place, the words washed away under the stark white fluorescent lights.

Around the room, kids socialize. But I keep my head down. I evenly space my five mechanical pencils and full-sized eraser in a neat line. I try to breathe.

Everyone here is the competition.

"You okay, Rahul?" Mr. Hayden comes up behind me.

"Yup." I keep my eyes focused on the desk.

"You know there's still ten minutes before this starts, right?"

"Uh-huh." I let out a slow exhale.

"You don't want to hang with the rest of the team?"

"I'm okay."

Mr. Hayden squats down next to me. "Hey, whatever happens today, I'm really proud of you kids."

"I know."

The test is hard. So much harder than districts. I've gnawed my lip raw and my fingers are tired from gripping my pencil. Pink eraser dust covers my desk.

"Ten minutes left," the moderator calls from the front of the room. Words from the projector morph into strange shapes across her face.

Question 23. Noura finds a metal disk . . . Smooshed behind a cube . . . In a box . . . The corner . . . The angle . . . What's the diameter?

I push my glasses up. I've got this.

And I do. The diameter is one inch.

Done. I grit my teeth. I work my way down the next six questions, each harder than the last, until I get to question thirty. The last question.

"Two minutes left."

Two minutes? I haven't double-checked anything.

AB and CD are parallel lines . . . Transversals intersect at a point between the lines . . .

I draw the lines. It's hard to keep track of them all.

"One minute."

More points lie on each segment . . .
The segments intersect . . .

"Thirty seconds."

What is the ratio?

Come on. Come on. Come on.

"Pencils down!"

A hand sweeps across my desk. My test gets picked up. That's it.

I silent-scream inside my head. I didn't finish, *and* I didn't double-check.

At lunch, it's like a repeat of districts. I can barely eat. But this time, I don't talk to anyone about how I did on the test at all.

Jenny doesn't say a word either.

I want so badly to know how she did. I want to know if she finished.

We're making our way down the long sidewalk to the engineering building for the Team Competition when I fall in step with her. We trail behind the rest of the group.

"Hey," I say.

"What's up?" she asks, and outside of a math formula, it's the first real thing she's said to me since the Sadie Hawkins dance.

"How'd you do?" I ask.

She raises a single shoulder.

"Did you finish?"

"Why do you care?"

We walk a few more feet in silence. The sun has gone behind the clouds now, and the sky is turning grayer by the minute.

"Are you mad at me?" I finally ask.

She stops, and the rest of our group is now too far ahead of us to notice we aren't following.

"Why did you go to the dance with me?" she asks.

"What do you mean? You asked me, and—"

"Yeah, but did you *want* to go with me?"

I'm not sure what I'm supposed to say.

"Or would you have rather just gone with Chelsea?"

"With Chelsea?" I ask.

"Rahul, you didn't even seem excited when I asked you. You had no interest in helping with the costumes. My mom and dad had to do everything. And, by the way, everyone liked them. And then, at the dance, you disappeared with Chelsea and took forever to come back!"

I just stand there, my mouth frozen open.

"No answer?"

I search my brain for something to say.

"Uh-huh. That's what I thought." She folds her arms across her chest and turns to walk away from me.

If she only knew what Chelsea and I were talking about.

If I could just tell her, maybe she wouldn't be so mad.

I watch as the group gets farther and farther away. Even though I'm positive now it wasn't Jenny who overheard us in the hallway, it doesn't make me feel any better.

We settle into our table for the Team Competition and Mr. Hayden gives us one last pep talk right before the moderator calls, "Go!"

We make it through the first nine questions okay, but question ten is a killer. *A fictional planet. Intergalactic stones in x, y, and z sizes. Meteor N. How many different combinations?*

We all work quietly on our own pieces of paper for a while. Then Jai says, "Did anyone else get 5,012?"

"I did." Jenny raises her hand.

I finish the last part of my multiplication. "I didn't. I got 6,008."

"I didn't get either of those," Gina says.

"Well, we're running out of time." Jai looks at the clock. Should we go with 5,012?"

"No, we should double-check our work." I flip over a blank sheet of paper.

"We *did* double-check." Jenny's voice is firm. "Two of us got the same thing. That's double-checking."

"I know, but *I* didn't get the same—"

"Well, why are you in charge, anyway?" she demands.

Before I can stop myself, I blurt out, "Because I won first place at districts!"

The team at the next table looks our way, and the monitor calls out, "Watch your voices please."

I try to cover. "I'm sorry. I didn't mean—"

"Wow." Gina puts her pencil down. "Just wow."

"Guys, go easy on him," Jai says. "He's just tired. He was up practicing all night."

"Sorry," I mumble. "Let's just go with what everyone else got."

The awards ceremony is in an old theater on campus. A giant red curtain drapes across the stage, and kids from all over the state are making their way into the velvet-covered seats.

"You guys all right?" Mr. Hayden asks as we climb over people's legs, looking for five seats together.

No one answers.

A woman from the engineering faculty comes onstage. She tells us she was a Mathlete when she was younger, and even placed second at the National Mathletics Competition.

And then they're announcing the winners.

Teams is first.

I lean forward in my seat and look down the aisle at the rest of the Greenville Junior High Mathletes.

I feel a hand grab my hand, and look up to see Jai smiling at me. On his other side, he's holding Gina's hand. And Gina is holding Jenny's. I guess whatever happens, we're still a team.

"Third place team goes to . . . Jackson Creek Middle School!"

A whoop goes up in the auditorium, and my stomach sinks a little. There are only two winning slots left. The team from Jackson Creek high-fives their teacher and heads back to their seats.

"In second place, we have . . . Kennedy-King Junior High!"

The roars are even louder now, and a few teachers

stand up to give the kids from Kennedy-King a standing ovation.

"And now. For our first place team . . ."

Before she can even finish the sentence, the screams become deafening. Kids are jumping up and down in front of their seats.

"This year's Indiana state champions . . ."

Jai's hand bears down on mine, and I press myself against the back of the seat so hard that my feet come off the floor. Please let us win.

"First place goes to . . ."

Come on. Come on. Come on.

"Memorial Park Junior High!"

A thunderous applause flies through the air and Jai's hand unfurls from mine as he leaps to his feet. In fact, the whole room is standing now.

I weakly push myself out of my chair and join in the clapping. But with each clap, I become more and more sure that I'm not going to win Individuals. We didn't even place in Teams. How could I possibly be going to nationals?

After what feels like an eternity, the room finally quiets down.

"Now we'll be acknowledging the top ten winners in the Individual round," the engineering teacher says. "Please come up as I call your name. And remember, the top four winners will get a trophy and go on to represent the state of Indiana at the National Competition."

I sink back into my seat, and when she calls out, "Fifth place, Rahul Kapoor, from Greenville Junior High!" I'm aware that my classmates are hugging me and screaming in my ear, and I feel my feet leave the floor for a second as Mr. Hayden twirls me around in the air and pushes me toward the stage. And I feel the heat of the footlights below me, and the cool skin of the engineering teacher's hand as she shakes mine. And I know it's my name I see in black calligraphy on the certificate next to the words *Fifth Place*. And I see the word after that, that says *Winner.*

But I don't feel like one.

CHAPTER 33

When we get home from states, Mom, Dad, Bhai, and Arun are piled inside Mom's minivan in the school parking lot, waiting to pick me up. It's raining buckets, and I have to quickly duck into the back seat to keep from getting drenched. I hand up my soggy certificate for everyone to pass around. "Fifth place? Out of the whole state? Wow!" Mom exclaims as she pulls out onto the road.

"I'm so proud!" Dad smiles back at me. "You were only one spot away from making the state team. That's fantastic!"

I press my head up against the window and stare outside.

My whole body feels numb.

It's over.

The next day, I wake up with a pit in my stomach, replaying it all over and over again in my head. The thundering applause. Applause that *wasn't* for me. How the four winners had jumped up and down in a circle, hugging each other. How they'd each gotten a turn at the mic to say something to the audience about what an honor it would be for them to represent the great state of Indiana.

On Monday, I beg Mom and Dad to let me stay home from school. I even concoct plans to convince them I'm sick, but when you have a dad who's a doctor, holding a thermometer next to a hot lightbulb and acting like you have a fever doesn't exactly cut it.

When Mr. Hayden announces my "win" at assembly, I see his mouth moving, but I can barely hear the words.

The rest of the school week is a total blur. Just one class after another, after another, after another. And then, finally, the week is over, and it's spring break. Which means I can hole myself up in my room and not deal with anyone.

Which is exactly what I do.

✦ ✦ ✦

I'm lying on my bed when the walkie-talkie on my nightstand springs to life.

"Rahul!" Bhai's voice calls. "Come down! Let's have lunch!"

"No thanks," I walkie back.

"Why not?" he pleads.

"I just want to be alone," I groan.

"It's just me. Nobody else is home." He makes his voice all singsongy. "We could have microwave pizza!"

Shoot. He knows how to work me.

I climb out of bed and head down the stairs. The house is eerily quiet.

"Where is everyone?" I ask, dropping into a chair at the kitchen table.

"It's Sunday," Bhai says, fishing the microwave pizza box out of the freezer. "Everyone's rehearsing at the school. And Arun went along to bother them."

"Why isn't Dad rehearsing in the garage?"

Bhai stops unwrapping the pizza box and narrows his eyes at me. "You remember the Bazaar is *next* weekend, right?"

"Yeah, of course I do," I say defensively. But the truth is, I've been so caught up with Mathletes that I'd completely forgotten it was almost time for the

Bizarre. I can't believe it's next weekend.

"So, since there are no classes at the school, they started taking all the Bazaar equipment over this week. And I think they're doing a dress rehearsal or something today."

"They need a whole *week* to set up?" I ask. "Why would it take a week?"

Bhai stares at the directions on the back of the microwave pizza box. "Shh. I need to concentrate."

"On what?"

"On cooking."

"It's *microwave* pizza, Bhai. How hard can it be?"

"Am I the chef, or are you the chef?"

"You're the chef," I mumble.

Bhai "cooks" the pizza.

"It says four minutes," he says, eyeing it as it slowly spins around inside the microwave, "but I don't trust them."

Exactly four minutes later, when we're eating the pizza, Bhai nudges me. "The sun is out today. We should play outside after lunch." He leans back in his wheelchair. "I see Mr. McCarter's Jeep is parked outside . . ."

"No thanks." I wipe a strand of cheese off my chin. "I have some stuff to do in my room."

"Like what?"

"Just stuff."

Bhai takes his napkin off his lap and sets it down on the table. "How come Chelsea never comes over anymore?"

Um, because Chelsea and I aren't talking, I think to myself.

"Rahul, is everything okay?"

No. No, it's not okay. I miss Chelsea. A lot. And I'm still confused about everything with Justin. And Jenny is mad at me. And if I never, ever see Brent ever, ever, ever again in my whole life, it would still be too soon. And I'm clearly never going to be the best at anything. Which means nothing will ever change. So what's the point?

"Everything is fine, Bhai!" I stand up. My voice comes out way louder than I'd expected. "Sorry. I didn't mean to raise my voice. Are you done? I'll do the dishes."

He leaves me alone at the sink. When I'm done washing the dishes, I turn off the faucet and run my hand under it five times. "Off, off, off, off, off," I whisper. Then I check the dials on the stove. "Off, off, off, off, off." I'm heading out of the kitchen when I feel paralyzed. Am I sure the stove is off? I want to go check it one more time, but I feel like if I do, I'll get stuck in here. Like every time I check something, as soon I turn around, I have to go back and check it again. And again. And again. Because no amount of checking will ever make that feeling go away. That feeling that something bad is going to happen if I don't check it one more time.

I bury my face in my hands, wishing it would stop.

"Rahul. Are you all right?" Bhai asks quietly from the doorway.

"Please just leave me alone!" I say. I run past him and up the stairs.

That night, I'm changing into my pajamas when there's a knock on my door.

"Go away, Arun!" I moan.

The door creaks open, and Dad peeks his head in. "Hey. Have a minute to talk?"

"Okay." I shrug, standing in the middle of the floor.

"Why is your bed out like that?" Dad asks. He walks in and starts to push my bed back up against the wall.

"No, no, no! Don't do that!" I beg, and my whole body starts to shake.

"Okay, okay," Dad says, shushing me with his hands. "But why? What's going to happen if I do?"

And because I know *nothing* is going to happen . . .

Because I know, in all the years that I've had this bed, it has *never* caught on fire from being close to the outlet . . .

Because, even though I know that, I also believe that somehow, just somehow, it *might* happen, and I have to keep it from happening . . .

Because I don't know how to explain that to Dad, or even understand it myself . . .

Because this whole school year I feel like I've been carrying around a weight too huge to bear . . .

Because I'm tired, tired, tired . . .

I start to cry.

Dad walks over to me. "I'm sorry. I didn't mean to move it." He wraps his arms around me until I stop shaking so much. "It's okay, Rahul." He guides me over to the bed, and we both sit down. "We'll leave the bed where it is, okay?"

"Okay," I say, wiping away the tears on my cheeks.

He gives me a minute, and then he gently says, "Bhai told me he sees you checking the stove sometimes. And the front door. Is that kind of the same thing as the bed?"

"I don't know," I mumble.

"Do you want to talk about it?" Dad asks.

I pick at the comforter. "Not really."

We sit there for a while. Dad stares at the floor like he wants to say something, but he's quiet for a long time.

Then finally, he clears his throat.

"Rahul." He runs a hand through his hair and lets it rest on the back of his neck for a moment. "Your mom and I know that you've been under a lot of stress lately. We can see it. Mom says you're tired in the mornings. She thinks you aren't sleeping well." He pauses. "We both want to help you, but . . . You see, as a parent, you wish you had all the answers. But, sometimes, as much as you hate it, you just don't."

Then he smiles down at me. "Did you know that? That Mom and I don't know everything? I mean, you probably think we're perfect. And that we're the coolest parents in the world . . ."

I sniffle out a little laugh.

"Oh, what? We're *not* the coolest parents?"

"You guys are all right." I smile back at him.

He puts a hand on my back. "Rahul, what I'm trying to say is, your mom and I want to help you, but we're not sure *how* to help you. So, we were thinking . . ." He hesitates, rubbing his hand on his thigh. "Well, I have a colleague at the hospital. Dr. Sanders. He said it might be a good idea for you to come talk to him. Mom and I could go with you, or you could go on your own. But we think he might be able to help you."

My eyes start to water again. "Is something wrong with me?"

"No. No, Rahul, nothing is wrong with you. Listen, it's only if you want."

"But you mean a therapist, right?"

"He's a therapist, yes."

"But doesn't that mean that something's wrong with me?"

"No. It doesn't. I mean it. What he told me is that this behavior, like when you check things, is just something in the way your brain works. You get an idea that something bad might happen and then you think you have to do things—like check the locks or check the stove or pull the bed away from the wall—to keep that bad thing from happening. The problem is that once you start checking, you have to keep checking. Over and over and over again. Everybody's brain is different. But it doesn't mean there's anything wrong with you. And, Rahul, I think he can help you understand why you're doing it, and help you learn how to make it better."

I swallow. My body relaxes a bit just knowing that somebody might understand. That I might not be the only person in the world who feels this way.

"Is it because I've been so stressed?" I ask.

"Well, he did say that stress can make it worse. Can trigger it." Dad looks at me. "Do you know why you've been so stressed lately?"

I think about all the things I'm hiding, pushing away, all the things I don't like about myself. How I thought being the best at something would make all that go away. How hard I've been trying to win, and how bad it feels to lose.

But I just say, "I don't know."

Dad pats my back. "That's okay. But I think Dr. Sanders might be able to help you talk about it. Do you think you'd like to meet him?"

I take a deep breath. "Can I think about it?"

"Of course."

"And you and Mom will come with me, if I want?"

"One hundred percent."

I look over at my alarm clock. I follow the cord to where it disappears behind my bed. I think about how many times I've waved my hand between the bed skirt and the outlet.

I nod. "Okay. I think I probably should."

Dad tightens his hand on my shoulder and gives me a little squeeze. "Good. I'll make an appointment for us. For all of us." He stands up. "Do you think you'll be okay tonight? With the bed?"

"Yeah."

"If you need anything, you know you can wake us up, okay?"

He starts toward the door and then hesitates. He turns back around. "Rahul. Whether you place first or fifth or thirty-fifth or two thousand and fifth . . ." He pauses, and he looks me right in the eye. "And no matter *who you are.* Your mom and I will always love you."

CHAPTER 34

After Dad leaves, I dare myself to push the bed a tiny bit closer to the wall. Not all the way back to where it was, but just a little closer. I sit on the floor and stare at the space between the bed and the wall for a while, and the next thing I know, it's morning.

I'm not excited to go to a therapist. Honestly, I don't want to go at all. But then, Dad sets up a call so I can meet Dr. Sanders over the phone, and when he says, "I'll see you next week. You're a brave young man, Rahul," I feel a flutter of something. Something better than I've felt in a while.

I'd planned on spending the week of spring break sulking in my room, but instead the time off gives me a chance to think about things. About Chelsea. And Justin. And Brent. And Jenny. And Jai. And Gina. And David.

And me.

And before I know it, the week is over and it's the day of the Bazaar.

"Come on, Rahul!" Bhai bellows through my walkie-talkie. "Everyone's already in the car!"

I'm standing in my room, still dripping wet in my towel, trying to get dressed. "I'm coming!" I walkie back. I glance from the jeans I've laid out on the bed to the Indian clothes Mom's set out on my dresser.

"Ugh, why not?" I say to myself.

I hurry down the stairs.

"Oh ho, very nice!" Bhai beams as we head out the front door. "You wore your kurta!"

"Don't get too excited," I say, smiling. "Mom insisted."

It's ridiculous how nice it is out. The sun beats down on our driveway, and the birds are going nuts. Spring is definitely here.

Dad's loading a few trays of food into the minivan and singing under his breath.

"Wait. Are you humming Pink?" I ask incredulously.

"Maybe." Dad slams the trunk shut.

"Why do Rahul and I have to wear these?" Arun asks, tugging on his white kurta.

"Because you both look so handsome in them." Mom ushers him into the back seat. I stick my tongue out as I buckle up next to him.

Mom gathers up the hem of her sari and pulls the driver's-side door shut behind her.

"Everyone ready?" she asks. She winks at me in the rearview mirror and starts up the minivan.

The football field has been transformed for the International Bazaar. On one end is a giant stage framed by towering scaffolding. Huge lights and enormous speakers dangle over the stage at dangerous angles, and the whole setup is flanked by two stadium-sized jumbotrons.

I can't believe it. This is nothing like last year.

On both sides of the field, the sun gleams down on table after table covered with food, each table topped with a banner advertising specialties from around the world. The plastic tablecloth at the Thai Tanic booth is hidden under rows and rows of spring rolls, and heaps of yellow rice and black beans fill steel bowls under the Here Today, Gone Tamale sign.

Arun and I each carry a tray of food as we follow Mom over to the India-Na Chutney booth. Nandita Auntie comes running out to greet us. "Get it?" she says. "India *and* Indiana! India-NA Chutney. So good, right?" She does a grand sweep with both her arms. "Can you believe it, Sarita? We did it! This will be the biggest Bazaar ever! We are putting Greenville on the map!

"Rahul! Arun!" She pinches our cheeks as Arun and I set our food trays down on the table. "You both wore your kurtas! And you wore white! Very good! Very good!"

"Why is it good they're white?" I ask.

Mom and Nandita Auntie exchange a knowing glance.

"You ask too many questions!" Nandita Auntie feigns annoyance. "You'll find out later!"

Juhi Auntie pops up from behind the table, two cardboard box lids in her hand. "So, I should try to keep these hidden?" she whispers.

Arun and I peer over the table. There, tucked away in boxes, are what look like hundreds of mini water balloons and little plastic packets filled with powder in every color of the rainbow.

"Wait!" I turn to Mom. "Are we playing—?"

"Shh! Never mind!" Mom cuts me off. "Yes, Juhi, please keep those covered!"

Arun's eyes are popping out of his head. "Can we play with those now?"

"Later!" Nandita Auntie blocks the booth. "First comes food. And then, if you're a good boy, maybe you can play."

"Well hello, everyone!" Mr. Wilson comes walking over. Chelsea's right behind him. I feel like I haven't seen her in ages.

"Oh, hi, Chelsea," Nandita Auntie squeals. "Are you excited for the performance?"

Mom gives her a big hug. "You're going to be great!" she says with a sly smile. She shakes hands with Mr. Wilson.

"Okay, okay, everyone in this group is too skinny! Let's go see all the food!" Nandita Auntie starts corralling everyone toward the rest of the booths. "Come on Juhi!"

Mr. Wilson kisses Chelsea on the forehead, saying, "Break a leg!" He hands her a duffel bag and then heads off with the aunties, leaving Chelsea and me alone for a minute.

"Hi," I say.

"Hi." She puts a hand over her eyes, shielding them from the sun.

"Chels—"

"Ra—"

We both start talking at the same time. We pause.

Then, we both say, "You first," at the same time again.

"Sorry, you." It happens again.

"Okay, this is ridiculous," she laughs. "What? Just say it."

I look her in the eyes and take a deep breath. "I'm so sorry, Chels."

She nods. "Me too."

And even though I don't think she needs to apologize, and even though I haven't even told her what it is I'm sorry for, just like that it's all over. Turns out saying sorry isn't that hard. Especially to your best friend in the whole world.

"Bustin' out the Indian clothes, huh?" She looks me up and down with a smile. "Nice."

"You think?" I ask, taking in her jeans and T-shirt. The slightest panic hits me now that we're actually here. All my classmates are going to see me in this.

She waves across the field, and I turn to look. "It's Trina and her parents. Let's go say hi!"

"Since when are you friends with Trina?" I ask.

"Um, since we decided to do something at the Bazaar together."

"You and Trina are doing something?" I realize just how long it's been since Chelsea and I really talked. "What exactly are you guys doing, anyway?" I ask as we make our way over. People are trickling in now, and the place is really starting to fill up. It's like everyone in the whole town of Greenville plus three more cities is here. I guess Mom and the Auntie Squad really made it happen.

"You'll see," she says.

Before we make it to Trina, I hear a voice calling, "Hey, my Mathlete brotha!" I turn to see Jai waving at us. He's with Jenny, Gina, and David. We stop and wait for them to come to us.

"Look at you, my man!" Jai says, putting his hands on my shoulders and spinning me around. "Mr. India! *Wah, wah!* Even I'm not wearing my kurta!"

We slap each other a low five, and then I quietly say, "Hey, Jenny." But she keeps her head down, no eye contact. Gina and David are asking Chelsea about her spring break when out of the corner of my eye I see Brent and Justin walking up to Trina and her parents.

My stomach clenches.

And it clenches even tighter when Trina calls, "Chelsea!" and starts to head our way with Brent and Justin in tow.

I let out a slow breath, and Chelsea nudges me. "Don't worry about him. We're all here together."

Now they're just a few feet away. I don't know if I'm ready for this.

"Are you so excited?" Trina gushes. She and Chelsea clasp hands and get all giggly.

I feel so uncomfortable.

"Why are you dressed like that?" Brent points at me.

"Hey, everyone," Justin says to the whole group before Brent can say any more.

There's a round of awkward hellos between people who normally don't hang out together, and everyone comments on all the food and how big the stage is. But my mouth feels frozen shut.

Then, Brent asks again, "Seriously, why are you dressed like that?"

Gina and David exchange glances.

"It's a traditional Indian outfit," Jai says. "So, it's actually perfect for today."

"Huh. Like, from India?" Justin tilts his head back to look at me. "That's cool."

"It's *cool*?" Brent snorts.

"Yeah." Justin shrugs. "I think so."

"Um, okay." Brent cuts him off, his eyes widening in amazement. "Well, I guess Rahul can die happy now. Now that you think he looks *cool*."

"Excuse me?" Chelsea cuts in.

"Die happy?" Justin rolls his eyes. "What are you even talking about?"

"Rahul knows what I'm talking about. I mean, I heard him tell Chelsea. Right, Rahul? At Sadie Hawkins?" Brent stares at me. "All about your big ol' crush on Justin."

Jenny turns to me, a question mark in her eyes.

So it *was* Brent in the hallway. Of course it was. Why is he *always* on me? Why does he care so much?

Justin turns to Brent. "Brent," he says evenly. "Whatever you're doing, just stop it."

"Don't tell me what to do," Brent says, and then to everyone's surprise, he shoves Justin. Trina gasps as Justin falls back a few steps. "Why do you always defend him anyway?"

Justin steadies himself and looks at Brent. "What exactly is your problem? What do you mean, defend him?"

"You know what I mean. Cheering for him in convo? Going to auditions with him? Rahul this, Rahul that. What's your deal?" Brent pushes him again. Harder.

I feel like I'm going to be sick. I just want all of this to stop.

Now Justin pushes Brent back, and Brent's foot must get caught, because he stumbles and falls backward onto the ground. "Stop pushing me," Justin says. "Rahul's my friend. I've known him forever. What's *your* deal?"

Brent springs back up and rushes Justin, throwing his arms around his waist. Everyone in our group gets tense. But no one moves.

"You know what my deal is?" Brent grunts, and now Justin is doubled over on top of him, trying to pry him off. The veins in Brent's neck are bulging, and the side of his face is pressed up against Justin's stomach. "Everyone here knows it, but no one will say it!" He tries to pull Justin to the ground. "Everyone knows that Rahul's—"

Before he can finish, Justin flips Brent over, and

now they're rolling around on the grass, heaving and moaning, their arms and legs tangled together.

And then I scream, "STOP IT!" I close my eyes and jump on top of them. I feel the heat of their bodies and blades of grass on my arms and the fabric of their shirts against my cheeks, and I'm expecting it to hurt, or to get punched in the face, and so I just keep screaming, "STOP IT! STOP IT! STOP IT!" as if all the screaming might protect me.

Until, finally, Brent and Justin roll away onto the grass next to me.

I'm breathing so hard, and adrenaline is coursing through my whole body, but somehow I manage to stand up and look Brent right in the eye. "Everybody knows that I'm what?" I say, my chest heaving up and down. But even though I'm still catching my breath, my voice comes out surprisingly clear. "That I'm—"

Chelsea raises a cautious hand. "Rahul, you don't have to say anything you don't want to. Brent can't force you to—"

"It's okay, Chels." I keep my eyes on Brent. "Everybody knows that I'm what?"

His nostrils flare in and out.

"That I'm gay? Is that what you want to hear? That I'm gay?"

The only sound is the three of us breathing. The laughter and voices from the Bazaar feel like they're a million miles away.

Then Brent turns to look at Justin expectantly. Like now that I've said it, Justin will side with him or something. But instead, Justin just shrugs, sweat trickling down his cheek.

And when Brent looks back up at me, I see the weirdest expression on his face. I'm not sure if it's betrayal or anger or embarrassment.

Then his whole face crumples and he tears off toward the entrance of the football field as though his life depends on it.

We all stand there, stunned. And then Chelsea takes my hand. "Hey," she says softly. "Do you want to get cleaned up?"

I look down at my white kurta, covered in grass stains and dirt, and I nod.

"Proud of you, Rahul," Jai says as we walk by him. Jenny reaches out and squeezes my arm. David shoots me a thumbs-up, Gina pats my shoulder, and Trina blows me a kiss.

CHAPTER 35

"Well, this settles it. It's not just the one by your locker. Every single boys' bathroom at this school is officially disgust-a-mundo." Chelsea hands me a paper towel, and I dampen it in the sink and scrub away at the grass stains on my kurta.

"You'd think they'd at least have cleaned the one by the football field for all the guests today. I mean, right?" She looks around, appalled.

"Should we talk about what just happened?" I interrupt her.

"You mean how awesome you were, or do you mean Brent running away like that?"

"I mean Brent."

"I know. How weird was that?"

Maybe it was just the pressure of all of us staring at him, but I can't help wondering if Brent has something he might be hiding, too. If maybe we have more in common than I could have ever thought.

"Are you thinking what I'm thinking?" Chelsea asks.

"Uh-huh," I say, nodding. "At least, I'm pretty sure I am."

She grows quiet. "If he is . . . I mean, if Brent is gay, can you imagine him having to tell his dad? I mean, *Mr. Mason*? I wouldn't wish that on anyone."

I remember when Dad came into my room, and the words he said are seared in my brain: "Rahul. Whether you place first or fifth or thirty-fifth or two thousand and fifth . . . And no matter *who you are*. Your mom and I will always love you."

"Maybe we're giving him too much credit," Chelsea says. "I mean, maybe he's just a jerk."

"Maybe."

She hands me another paper towel, and I look down at myself. "Um, Chels, I don't think these grass stains are coming out. I think I'm just gonna have to be a little bit messy today."

I toss the paper towels in the trash can.

"Finally!" Chelsea smiles. "A boy who knows how to use a garbage can!"

From outside, we hear the muffled sounds of music coming through the speaker system. Chelsea clutches her duffel bag and gasps. "Ah! I have to change." She runs into a stall and slams the door shut. She squeals, "Oh my God, it smells so bad in here I'm going to barf!" Then I hear an endless amount of rustling mixed in with little eruptions like, "Ew, gross! My foot touched the floor!"

Finally, the stall door flings open and Chelsea emerges in a silver sequined leotard and tights.

"What *exactly* are you doing today?" I ask.

"I've got to hurry!" She digs through her bag and pulls out a sparkly tube of lip balm. "Trina insisted I wear this." She heads over to the mirror, but it's rusted and dirty, and I can tell she can't see anything in it.

"Here, let me help you." I grab the stick out of her hand and dip the glittering tip of it into the container.

"Do you think it's strange we always end up in boys' bathrooms doing each other's makeup?" She puckers her lips.

"Absolutely not," I say with a smile. "Being different is what makes us fun, remember?"

CHAPTER 36

The Bazaar is in full force when we emerge outside. Chelsea takes off toward the stage, and I head over to the food stalls.

I pile up a plate of Ethiopian *azifa* salad, Vietnamese *banh it tran*, and even a slice of pizza from Italy. And of course, I top it all off with a samosa from India.

I head over to the stage by myself and try not to make a mess as I eat the *banh it tran*. Warm mung-bean filling drips over my fingers and almost misses my plate. Onstage, a mariachi band is finishing up their set.

A round of applause goes up as they walk off the

stage, and Nandita Auntie whizzes out to take the podium. "Weren't they just wonderful?" She waves at the mariachi band. "Now for our next act, I invite you to come with us to my motherland . . ." She takes a dramatic pause. "Indiaaaa!" She nods at the wings, and I see Dad rolling his head around and stretching out his tongue. "Please put your hands together for Bollywood Supply!" Nandita Auntie beckons them onstage, and the crowd starts whooping and applauding. "Now, pay attention, because they have a very special announcement to make!"

Dad, Vinay Uncle, and Jeet Uncle come out and set up their instruments. And weirdly, I don't feel nervous about Dad singing at my school. A surge of pride goes through me when he spots me in the audience and waves.

He leans into his mic. "Thanks, Nandita. We're Bollywood Supply, and we're thrilled to be here with you. We have a great act planned for you today, but before we begin, we also have a little surprise. To share the joy of India, we thought the Bazaar would be the perfect opportunity to play Holi, the Indian festival of colors."

I knew it! I knew that's what all those boxes were for!

"See, the festival of Holi celebrates the triumph of good over evil, the coming of spring after winter, and the chance to forgive people and repair relationships."

"Don't forget to tell them about the balloons!" Nandita Auntie shouts, and her eagerness makes the audience giggle.

"Right," Dad says. "We celebrate Holi by dousing each other with all the colors of the rainbow. We use colored powders and water balloons filled with colored water. I think you'll get the hang of it pretty quickly."

There's some more whooping, and I can tell that people are intrigued.

"But before we get to that, how about some music, huh?" Dad strums a chord on his guitar, and the crowd erupts with applause.

Mom runs onstage to meet Nandita Auntie. They both match in their glittering, colorful *chaniya* cholis. They strike a pose, one hand on a hip, one arm up in the air. Their heads are turned to the side and angled down, but I see Mom wink at Nandita Auntie, and they look so young. I don't think I've ever seen them this excited. The rest of the Auntie Squad files into a semicircle behind them.

"When we started practicing for the Bazaar many months ago," Dad says, "we had our hearts set on singing an Air Supply song but giving it a Bollywood spin. But sometimes, what you think are the best-laid plans are the very plans you need to change.

"So here's to the Golden Age of Bollywood!" He nods down to the DJ booth at the front of the stage and then plucks out the first few strains of "Yeh Dosti" on his guitar.

Wait, they're playing my favorite song?

Dad and Bollywood Supply hit every note on key as the Auntie Squad owns the stage, feet pounding the ground, shoulders bobbing every which way, wrists twirling around in the air. I'm smiling so hard my face hurts.

Bhai wheels up to me. "What do you think?" he laughs, and we sing along like we're in the movie *Sholay*, except this time I'm in the motorcycle and he's in the sidecar, and I think I've never been happier in my life.

Then the DJ starts to fill in under Dad, and now Bollywood Supply is being backed up by hard-core beats, and the whole audience starts dancing along.

Then the music shifts, and the aunties throw up an "Oh ho!" on stage, and now Dad and the band and the DJ are rolling from one Bollywood song into the next.

I grin down at Bhai. They're doing a medley of Bhai's greatest hits!

Just when I think it can't get better, Chelsea and Trina run out in their sequined leotards. They fall in step with the Auntie Squad, matching Bollywood move after Bollywood move, their hands in prayer, then up over their heads. Chelsea and Trina spinning in a circle.

Until the music shifts again, and I hear the chorus of Pink's "What About Us."

No WAY! IT'S A MASH-UP!

My pulse is thumping with excitement as this time the Auntie Squad falls in step with Chelsea and Trina, Mom and the aunties throwing down some rockin' dance moves.

Chelsea really did it, I think. She found a way to bring two cultures together.

There is no way I'm missing out on this next year.

I'm dancing my head off when a water balloon smacks me in the chest and explodes colors all over my shirt. I turn to see Arun standing next to a cardboard box filled with artillery. Holi is starting! He lobs another balloon our way, and Bhai sneaks a hidden one out of his sweater pocket and chucks it back.

"My secret stash. I've got to reload!" Bhai chortles, wheeling himself away.

Now, everyone around me is in on it, and it seems like the whole world is an explosion of color. Powders and water balloons sail through the air. People smear each other's faces with hands covered in gooey, wet powder. And I'm standing in the center, watching it all.

"This stuff is awesome! Aren't you gonna play?" A shower of colored powder rains down on the back of my neck, and I turn to see Justin, his white polo swirling in every color of the rainbow.

"Yeah. In a minute." I smile. My breath catches because I know there are still some things I should probably say to him.

"Hey Justin," I call over the music. "About what happened back there. What Brent said." It feels so awkward to say this. "I don't have a crush on you—" Oh boy. What am I even saying? What *is* my deal with Justin? I still don't think I understand it. "I guess I'm just trying to say, I just want to be your friend."

Justin bobs his head up and down. "Okay. Cool.

Me too." Then he furrows his brow. "Hey, you didn't stop hanging out at my house just 'cause you're gay, did you?"

"Wait. What? You think *I* stopped hanging out with *you*?"

"Well, didn't you?"

"No! I mean we both just . . ."

Someone's water balloon smacks me in the back, and before I can pick up where I left off, Justin does the weirdest wolf howl, which makes me wonder why I ever thought he was so cool in the first place, and yells, "You better go get some ballooooooons!"

And then he's gone.

"Everything all right?" Chelsea comes up behind me, still flushed from just having finished her dance.

I turn and smile. "Definitely." I reach behind my neck and get colored powder all over my fingers. "Happy Holi!" I shriek as I smear my hand across her face. "YOU WERE SO AWESOME UP THERE!"

Then we BRiC it so hard, it's like our hands are actual fireworks.

CHAPTER 37

The driveway is glowing in the moonlight when we get home from the Bazaar. Mom turns off the van and Dad carries a passed-out Arun into the house while I get Bhai's wheelchair out of the back.

We're all still drenched in colors, so when we get inside, I head upstairs to shower. I peel off my kurta and look at myself in the bathroom mirror. My brown skin is smeared in every shade of the rainbow. I smile at my reflection. My braces smile back at me.

I take a shower, and then I head downstairs. Mom, Dad, and Bhai are in the living room drinking tea and laughing. My stomach flips, and I'm tempted to just forget about the whole thing and go to bed. But somehow I summon up the courage to keep going.

"Hey, can I come in?" I hesitate in the entryway.

"Of course." Dad pats the sofa next to him. "What is it, Rahul?"

Somehow, this feels scarier than standing up to Brent on the football field.

I take a deep breath as I settle into the sofa between Mom and Dad. "I want to tell you something," I say.

"Okay," Mom says. "You can tell us anything."

Bhai nods at me, and his eyes are bright. Encouraging.

I nod back.

"What is it, Rahul?" Mom gently rubs my back.

Even though I want to keep my eyes fixed on my lap, I force myself to lift my head up. My eyes water, but the words come out of my mouth so simply.

"I think I'm gay," I say.

I look up at Mom, and I see her whole face soften. Like she's proud of me.

She leans in and hugs me. "Thank you for telling us, Rahul."

I hold her for a long time.

We all talk pretty late into the night. I tell them that I'd overheard them worrying about what people like Vinay Uncle would think, and Dad assures me, "Don't worry about Vinay Uncle. He puts on a tough show, but I can handle him. Let him spend one afternoon in the ER with me, and I guarantee you he'd pass out on the spot!"

And before I head up the stairs, Mom needles me in the ribs. "Even if it means she has to find you a boy now, you know your Nandita Auntie's still going to try to marry you off!"

I'm finally getting into bed when my walkie-talkie crackles to life.

"Bhai to Rahul, do you copy?" it spits at me.

"Copy. This is Rahul. Go." I whisper back.

"I saw you at the Bazaar today," he says. "With your friends. I almost came over when all that fighting started. I was worried about you."

"Yeah?"

"But then I saw you stand up. I couldn't hear what you were saying, but I could see in your body how strong you were. How confident you were. And I knew everything was all right. Do you know why?"

"Why?"

"Because you reminded me of someone."

His voice breaks a little, like he's holding back tears, and I picture my grandmother's face.

"Rahul, in my book you have always been the best." He pauses. "You know that, right?"

But I don't know if I knew that. So I sit there, quiet, until Bhai says, "You taught me something today, Rahul."

Even though he can't see me, I shake my head just a little. I've always looked up to Bhai. How could *I* teach *him* something?

"You know how much I like to win, right?" he chuckles, and it makes me smile. "I mean, it's fun to win. But winning isn't everything. You don't have to prove yourself to anyone. You're already the best, Rahul, because you're you."

I hold the walkie up against my cheek for a second. Then I whisper, "I love you, Bhai," and set it back down in its cradle.

I think about what it means to be the best. How trying to had seemed like such a good idea at first.

I mean, I'm good at math. Really, *really* good at math. But I don't know if just because I'm good at it, I have to prove to everyone that I'm the best at it. A lot of Mathletes was fun, but I also made a lot of it way too stressful.

Maybe Chelsea's right. Maybe being the best is about finding something you love and doing it until you get better at it.

Or maybe . . . maybe it's something else entirely.

I look around my room, and with the moonlight streaming through my window, I can just make out my rainbow-soaked kurta thrown over the back of my chair, my thumbed-through copy of *Football for Dummies* on the bookshelf, that folded-up bank flyer tossed on my desk, and a stack of old practice tests shoved in my garbage can.

I lie back in my bed, which is still a few inches away from the wall, and pull the covers up around me. I close my eyes.

To my surprise, I can feel my whole face smiling.

ACKNOWLEDGMENTS

There aren't enough ribbons, medals, or trophies in the world.

Saira Rao and Carey Albertine at In This Together Media, thank you for saying, "Hey. Ever thought of writing a book?" and then giving me the courage, guidance, and resources to do just that.

Jessica Regel at Foundry Literary + Media, thank you for championing both me and this book from day one and for so thoughtfully finding the perfect home for it at Balzer + Bray. Richie Kern at Foundry, thank you for already looking to the next steps. And to my managers, Jai Khanna and Colton Gramm at

Brillstein Entertainment Partners, thank you for the constant support.

To everyone at Balzer + Bray/HarperCollins, you have all been a dream. There is an extraordinary amount of work that goes into making a book and getting it into the world—copyediting, proofreading, designing, marketing, publicizing, selling—and you have all gone above and beyond. Donna Bray, Suzanne Murphy, Caitlin Johnson, Andrea Pappenheimer, Kerry Moynagh, Kathy Faber, Nellie Kurtzman, Vaishali Nayak, Mitchell Thorpe, Cara Llewellyn, David DeWitt, Mark Rifkin, and Liz Byer, thank you.

To my editor, Alessandra Balzer, I am forever grateful to you for loving this book, loving these characters, and helping me find the real heart of this story. You have the uncanny ability to know exactly which notes need to sing a little louder and which parts of the score are already playing in the silence. You have been such an incredible creative partner—not to mention every other aspect of this process that you have managed—and I am so honored you took this book under your wing.

Parvati Pillai, the cover you illustrated is so

gorgeous and perfectly captures this book. I can't thank you enough.

Shobha Auntie, one of the original aunties, thank you for the Hindi help.

There were a few early readers of the book whose input was very valuable to me: Dr. Clayton Guthrie, thank you for providing such deep insight into Rahul's compulsive behaviors; Lila Govindan, thank you for your candor and inquisitiveness; my sister-in-law Erin and my nephew Cyrus, thank you for the perspective; and a big thanks to my cousin Manisha and my nephews Roshan and Nayan, who read the book once and then said they'd like to read it one more time so they could really hone their notes.

Soman Chainani, Anne Ursu, Kacen Callender, and John Schu, thank you for your early support of the book and your very kind words.

I've been inspired by so many people along the way, but a few are worth noting in relation to this story: Dr. Thom Morris, for being that teacher every kid should have and for making me a Mathlete, Nicole Vanderbilt, for being the best friend every middle schooler needs, Kathi Grau, for shepherding me into the arts, and Steve Heyman, for saying, "You can."

To everyone in my enormous, big-hearted family—all my cousins, nephews, nieces, masa, masi, mamis—thank you for being there for me and celebrating me. Dad, thank you for always encouraging me to reach higher.

And a most special thank-you to my Mom and sister. Mom, thank you for teaching me to hold my head up high and to be fearless in standing up for what's right. Your imprint is all over this book. Sona, thank you for always being the person I can turn to no matter what. The two of you have taught me what family can be, and I hope I have modeled that in this story.

And to my grandparents, Bhai and Ba, this book is a love letter to the both of you. I'm so lucky for all you instilled in me. I'm grateful for the conversations we were able to have, and I hope this book continues the ones we no longer can. I miss you immensely.

And finally, to my husband, Ryan, thank you for letting me interrupt you at any hour of the day, and sometimes night, to ask you if I should change a line. And for so patiently listening, even though you probably knew I'd end up just leaving it the way it is. There's a metaphor in there somewhere for our relationship . . . but I guess I'm just saying, we're a great team.